The Zuni

Indians of North America

Heritage Edition

Indians
of North
America

The Apache

The Arapaho

The Blackfeet

The Cherokees

The Cheyenne

The Choctaw

The Comanche

The Hopi

The Iroquois

The Mohawk

The Navajo

The Pawnee

The Teton Sioux

The Zuni

Heritage Edition

◀ **Indians** ▶
◀ **of North** ▶
◀ **America** ▶

The Zuni

Nancy Bonvillain

Foreword by
Ada E. Deer
University of Wisconsin–Madison

CHELSEA HOUSE
PUBLISHERS
A Haights Cross Communications ► Company ®

Philadelphia

COVER: A Zuni kachina doll that represents Heheya (lightning), Colorado Historical Society, Denver, Colorado.

CHELSEA HOUSE PUBLISHERS

VP, NEW PRODUCT DEVELOPMENT Sally Cheney
DIRECTOR OF PRODUCTION Kim Shinners
CREATIVE MANAGER Takeshi Takahashi
MANUFACTURING MANAGER Diann Grasse

Staff for THE ZUNI

EXECUTIVE EDITOR Lee Marcott
EDITOR Christian Green
PRODUCTION EDITOR Bonnie Cohen
PHOTO EDITOR Sarah Bloom
SERIES AND COVER DESIGNER Keith Trego
LAYOUT EJB Publishing Services

First Printing

9 8 7 6 5 4 3 2 1

Library of Congress Cataloging-in-Publication Data

Bonvillain, Nancy.
  The Zuni / Nancy Bonvillain.
    p. cm. — (Indians of North America)
  Includes index.
  ISBN 0-7910-8594-5 (hardcover)
  1. Zuni Indians—History—Juvenile literature. 2. Zuni Indians—Social life and cus-
toms—Juvenile literature. I. Title. II. Indians of North America (Chelsea House
Publishers)
  E99.Z9B66 2005
  978.9004'97994—dc22
                              2005006508

Contents

Foreword

Ada E. Deer

American Indians are an integral part of our nation's life and history. Yet most Americans think of their Indian neighbors as stereotypes; they are woefully uninformed about them as fellow humans. They know little about the history, culture, and contributions of Native people. In this new millennium, it is essential for every American to know, understand, and share in our common heritage. The Cherokee teacher, the Mohawk steelworker, and the Ojibwe writer all express their tribal heritage while living in mainstream America.

The revised INDIANS OF NORTH AMERICA series, which focuses on some of the continent's larger tribes, provides the reader with an accurate perspective that will better equip him/her to live and work in today's world. Each tribe has a unique history and culture, and knowledge of individual tribes is essential to understanding the Indian experience.

Prior to the arrival of Columbus in 1492, scholars estimate the Native population north of the Rio Grande ranged from seven to twenty-five million people who spoke more than three hundred different languages. It has been estimated that ninety percent of the Native population was wiped out by disease, war, relocation, and starvation. Today there are more than 567 tribes, which have a total population of more than two million. When Columbus arrived in the Bahamas, the Arawak Indians greeted him with gifts, friendship, and hospitality. He noted their ignorance of guns and swords and wrote they could easily be overtaken with fifty men and made to do whatever he wished. This unresolved clash in perspectives continues to this day.

A holistic view recognizing the connections of all people, the land, and animals pervades the life and thinking of Native people. These core values—respect for each other and all living things; honoring the elders; caring, sharing, and living in balance with nature; and using not abusing the land and its resources—have sustained Native people for thousands of years.

American Indians are recognized in the U.S. Constitution. They are the only group in this country who has a distinctive *political* relationship with the federal government. This relationship is based on the U.S. Constitution, treaties, court decisions, and attorney-general opinions. Through the treaty process, millions of acres of land were ceded *to* the U.S. government *by* the tribes. In return, the United States agreed to provide protection, health care, education, and other services. All 377 treaties were broken by the United States. Yet treaties are the supreme law of the land as stated in the U.S. Constitution and are still valid. Treaties made more than one hundred years ago uphold tribal rights to hunt, fish, and gather.

Since 1778, when the first treaty was signed with the Lenni-Lenape, tribal sovereignty has been recognized and a government-to-government relationship was established. This concept of tribal power and authority has continuously been misunderstood by the general public and undermined by the states. In a series of court decisions in the 1830s, Chief Justice John Marshall described tribes as "domestic dependent nations." This status is not easily understood by most people and is rejected by state governments who often ignore and/or challenge tribal sovereignty. Sadly, many individual Indians and tribal governments do not understand the powers and limitations of tribal sovereignty. An overarching fact is that Congress has plenary, or absolute, power over Indians and can exercise this sweeping power at any time. Thus, sovereignty is tenuous.

Since the July 8, 1970, message President Richard Nixon issued to Congress in which he emphasized "self-determination without termination," tribes have re-emerged and have utilized the opportunities presented by the passage of major legislation such as the American Indian Tribal College Act (1971), Indian Education Act (1972), Indian Education and Self-Determination Act (1975), American Indian Health Care Improvement Act (1976), Indian Child Welfare Act (1978), American Indian Religious Freedom Act (1978), Indian Gaming Regulatory Act (1988), and Native American Graves Preservation and Repatriation Act (1990). Each of these laws has enabled tribes to exercise many facets of their sovereignty and consequently has resulted in many clashes and controversies with the states and the general public. However, tribes now have more access to and can afford attorneys to protect their rights and assets.

Under provisions of these laws, many Indian tribes reclaimed power over their children's education with the establishment of tribal schools and thirty-one tribal colleges. Many Indian children have been rescued from the foster-care system. More tribal people are freely practicing their traditional religions. Tribes with gaming revenue have raised their standard of living with improved housing, schools, health clinics, and other benefits. Ancestors' bones have been reclaimed and properly buried. All of these laws affect and involve the federal, state, and local governments as well as individual citizens.

Tribes are no longer people of the past. They are major players in today's economic and political arenas; contributing millions of dollars to the states under the gaming compacts and supporting political candidates. Each of the tribes in INDIANS OF NORTH AMERICA demonstrates remarkable endurance, strength, and adaptability. They are buying land, teaching their language and culture, and creating and expanding their economic base, while developing their people and making decisions for future generations. Tribes will continue to exist, survive, and thrive.

Ada E. Deer
University of Wisconsin–Madison
June 2004

1

The Middle Place

In the beginning, say the Zunis, the only being who lived was *Awonawilona*, a deity both male and female. Nothing else existed, except some fog and steam. Then Awonawilona created the clouds and waters from its breath, and the rest of the universe was formed.

The universe created by Awonawilona consists of nine layers. The earth, a large circular island surrounded by oceans, occupies the middle level. The lakes, rivers, and springs on the earth are connected to the oceans by underground linkages. The sky layer is an upside-down bowl of stone, resting above the earth. The other eight layers of the universe are each home to different kinds of animals, birds, and trees.

At first people lived under the earth's surface in the fourth and innermost layer of the universe, deep inside the body of Earth Mother. The people did not look like humans today. Instead their bodies were covered with slime, they had webbed hands and feet, and they had tails. They had no idea how strange they looked because it was dark where they lived and they could not see well. Then the Sun Father decided to bring the people out to the surface of the earth because he was lonely and had no one to give him offerings and prayers. Sun Father told his twin sons, the War Gods, to lead the Zunis out from inside the earth. The War Gods helped the people climb up a ladder to the surface of the earth and, once they were there, changed their appearance. The slime on the people's bodies disappeared and their hands and feet became normal. Deities and priests instructed the people to recite prayers, make offerings, and conduct ceremonies to honor Sun Father and other spirit powers. In return, the spirits gave people blessings and protection.

The Zunis remained near their place of emergence for a time. Then deities told the Zunis to go forth and find the middle place, or *itiwana*, of the world, where they should build their villages. Important holy men called Rain Priests led the people on a journey that took many years. Each time they chose a place to settle, some misfortune occurred that forced them to move again. These misfortunes were signs from the spirits that the people had not yet found the itiwana of the world.

At last the Zunis met an old man who was a powerful Rain Priest. When the Zunis' own Rain Priest prayed with the old man, a heavy rainstorm fell. Suddenly a water spider came by, spread out its six legs, and told the people that the itiwana was directly under its heart. The Zunis knew its message to be true and set about building their villages. They built one village at the itiwana and six others at locations marked off by the six legs of the water spider.

The Zunis then erected an altar at the exact site of the itiwana. On the altar they placed sacred objects belonging to the Rain Priests as reminders of the people's journey and of their duty to honor the powerful deities who led them there. The altar remains today at the center of the village of Zuni. On it rests a stone that contains the eternal beating heart of the itiwana of the world.

The Zunis' story of their creation, emergence, and discovery of the ĩtiwana situates them literally in the center of the world. Not surprisingly, they feel a strong spiritual and emotional connection to their locale. They and their ancestors lived for centuries in lands along the banks of the Zuni River in western New Mexico. Their beautiful homeland contains a diversity of terrain and resources, including flat plains, plateaus, deserts, woodlands, foothills, and mountains. On the plains and desert grasslands grow shrubs, herbs, cactus, rabbitbrush, and yucca. Oak, spruce, juniper, and piñon trees are abundant in woodlands and mountainous regions. The mountains and foothills are inhabited by many animals, such as elk, deer, antelope, mountain sheep, bears, and foxes. Rabbits, mice, squirrels, and reptiles abound in all areas.

Today the Zunis reside in one large town, called Zuni, and several small suburbs located along nearby rivers and streams. Before the arrival of Europeans in the early sixteenth century, the Zunis lived in six villages, all situated within a twenty-five-mile area and with access to good farmland. Zuni territory extended well beyond the area occupied by the villages, to the Zuni Mountains in the east and north, and the lower, more desertlike area to the west and south.

The Zunis made good use of the resources available in their territory, and their land has supported people from the time of the earliest arrival of their ancestors in the Southwest approximately ten thousand years ago. These early inhabitants created a civilization known to archaeologists as the Desert Tradition. Desert Tradition sites have been discovered at Concho in present-day eastern Arizona and at Bat Cave and Tularosa Cave in northern and central New Mexico. During the Desert period, people did not have permanent settlements. They shifted their camps from time to time, adjusting their settlements to changes in plant growth and animal populations. Due to the scarcity of permanent sources of food, Desert camps were small, consisting of no more than a few families. The Desert peoples hunted

(continued on page 6)

The Turkey Girl, A Zuni Narrative

"The Girl Who Took Care of the Turkeys" is a popular Zuni story. The Zunis traditionally kept flocks of domesticated turkeys, using the feathers to make ceremonial gear, that were tended by members of the family. There are many similarities between the Zuni story and the European story of Cinderella. Both tales have a central character who is a young woman wanting to go to a dance. Eventually, she does attend the dance, but is warned that she must be sure to return home early. In both stories, the girl stays later than the appointed time because she is enjoying herself.

The similarities between the two stories are no coincidence, but they also differ in significant ways. The Zunis first learned the Cinderella story from Americans in the 1880s and transformed it to make it consistent with their circumstances, values, and way of life. This is an example of borrowing that takes place when members of different cultures meet, share experiences, and learn from each other. Instead of a nameless European kingdom, the Zunis situate the tale in their own territory with references to specific villages, such as Wind Place and Middle Place. The aristocratic ball that Cinderella yearns to attend becomes the Yaaya Dance, an important Zuni festival. Consistent with the Zuni belief that four is a sacred number, the dance takes place over four days.

The Zunis also change the outcome of the story. Cinderella is virtuous and long suffering, and her stepmother and stepsisters force her to serve them and deprive her of her place at the ball. The girl in the Zuni story also serves as caretaker for her family, the flock of turkeys (whom she significantly addresses as "father" and "child"), but she is not seen as virtuous. On the contrary, she neglects her duties by staying at the dance, threatening the turkeys' well-being.

The stories also end very differently. Cinderella marries the handsome prince and lives happily ever after. No such good fortune befalls the Zuni girl. Her story ends badly because she thinks of her own pleasure before her responsibility to those under her care. The European story of individual virtue and fortitude rewarded has become a Zuni story of moral failing and the consequences of irresponsibility to one's relatives and dependents. As the turkey tells the girl, "You must think of us." The excerpt that follows picks up the story at the point where the Zuni girl has decided to attend the dance:

The next day the sun was shining, and she went among her turkeys and spread their feed. When she had fed them she said, "My fathers, my children, I'm going to the Middle Place. I'm going to the dance," she said. "Be on your way, but think of us . . ." That's what her children told her.

And she left. . . .

She went to where the place was, and when she entered the plaza, the dance directors noticed her.

Then they asked her to dance, she went down and danced, and she didn't think about her children.

Finally it was mid-day, and when mid-day came she was just dancing away until it was late, the time when the shadows are very long.

The turkeys said, "Our mother, our child doesn't know what's right."

"Well then, I must go and I'll just warn her and come right back and whether she hears me or not, we'll leave before she gets here," that's what the turkey said, and he flew away.

He flew along until he came to where they were dancing, and there he glided down to the place and perched on the top crotch piece of the ladder, and then he sang,

"Kyana tok tok Kyana tok tok."

The one who was dancing heard him.

He flew back to the place where they were penned, and the girl ran all the way back. When she got to the place where they were penned, they sang again, they sang and flew away. . .

When she came near they all went away and she couldn't catch up to them. Long ago, this was lived. . . .*

* Dennis Tedlock, *Finding the Center: Narrative Poetry of the Zuni Indians* (Lincoln, Nebr.: University of Nebraska Press, 1972), 67–72.

At the time of European contact in the mid-1500s, the Zunis lived in six villages—
Kiakima, Matsaki, Halona, Kwakina, Kechipauan, and Hawikuh—along the Zuni River
in western New Mexico. Today, most Zunis live in Zuni Pueblo, which, according to
the 2000 U.S. Census, has a population of 7,758. Shown here is a photo of the
pueblo in 1940.

(continued from page 3)

animals—including several species of now-extinct horses, ele-
phants, and great bison—for meat to use as food and for hides
to use for clothing and shelter. They also gathered wild plants
to eat and invented specialized technologies for preparing and
cooking plant foods. One such technology that has survived to
modern times is the use of *metates,* specialized grinding stones
for making meal of different kinds of seeds and nuts.

Thousands of years after Desert peoples first entered the
American Southwest, their descendants learned how to grow
some of their own food. The earliest evidence of farming in the
region dates from approximately five thousand years ago. The
Desert peoples apparently borrowed farming methods from
other *tribes* living farther south in present-day Mexico. These

techniques gradually spread into the present-day American Southwest through a process called cultural diffusion, the borrowing of skills by one group of people from neighboring groups.

The first plant grown by Native American farmers was corn—in fact, for approximately two thousand years corn was the only crop cultivated in America. Then, about three thousand years ago, Native American farmers began to cultivate varieties of beans and squash. These three plants—corn, beans, and squash—have remained staples of southwestern cuisine, including that of the modern Zunis. Although Desert peoples farmed, they combined farming with their earlier way of life, continuing to hunt animals, gather wild plants, and live in small nomadic groups. Then, in about 300 B.C., for reasons that remain unknown, a profound cultural change took place in the societies of the American Southwest. A new *culture* developed called the Mogollon Tradition. Mogollon peoples added many innovations to the older Desert Tradition, changing their settlements, economies, and technology.

The most obvious contrast between the Mogollon and Desert cultures is that Mogollon peoples lived in permanent villages. They built small settlements of approximately one hundred people, living in rectangular or circular houses made of clay and stone. Ruins of Mogollon villages have been found at Forestdale and Black River in Arizona and at Cibola and Mimbres in New Mexico.

Farming and agricultural products became more central to the lives and economies of the Mogollon peoples. Corn was prepared by first drying and crushing the kernels and then grinding them into meal using a grinding stone. The resulting cornmeal was moistened with water and cooked on heated stones. Fresh corn was also simply roasted over coals. Mogollon peoples dried beans to preserve them for later use; when they wanted to prepare the dried beans for meals, they soaked them and boiled them in water. Squash was either boiled in water when fresh or dried for later use. The seeds of squash, which are higher in calories, vitamins, and calcium than the flesh, were dried and stored for winter meals. In addition to the staples of corn, beans, and squash, the Mogollon peoples raised tobacco as well as cotton and sunflowers, which were cultivated for their vitamin- and calorie-rich seeds.

The Mogollon peoples expanded their inventory of tools and utensils. They made dishes, hammers, axes, hoes, bows, arrows, and a variety of grinding utensils, such as metates, mortars, and pestles from stone, wood, bone, and shell. Mogollon artists used tools to carve masks and effigies from stone and wood, while weavers used cotton (also introduced into the area by Mexican Indians) to make both plain and fancy cloth. In addition to these innovations, the Mogollon peoples began making earthen pottery, forming pots, bowls, and jars of different sizes and shapes to use for cooking and for carrying and storing foods and supplies.

By about A.D. 700 or 800 the Zunis' Mogollon ancestors had established permanent settlements in present-day Zuni territory. One such settlement is a village called White Mound, which contains groups of pit houses made of sandstone blocks and slabs and dug several feet into the ground to protect residents against outside cold and heat. In each house a series of rooms ten to twelve feet across is arranged in a line. A single nuclear family probably lived in each room, and a house probably contained a group of related families. In addition to the pit houses, storerooms were built at ground level to hold equipment and dried foods. Farmland was located outside the clusters of houses and storerooms.

Other Mogollon villages in present-day Zuni territory include Kiatuthlanna, built in A.D. 800 or 900. Kiatuthlanna was larger than White Mound; its eighteen homes held an estimated population of seventy-five to one hundred people. In a later village named Allantown, built around A.D. 1000, houses constructed at ground level had begun to replace pit houses as the typical form of residence. Allantown and other Mogollon villages also contained *kivas* (pronounced KEY-vas), special buildings where religious ceremonies were held.

Many innovative pottery designs, especially painted motifs, have been unearthed in Mogollon village digs. The artists initially used white paste and mineral paints to make black-on-white designs but eventually developed the use of glaze in the colors of green and cinnamon. The designs themselves also changed, from thin lines to wider and more blocky designs that included geometric shapes and naturalistic figures.

Another new culture developed in the American Southwest around A.D. 1100. Called the Anasazi Tradition, it covered a large area, including present-day New Mexico, most of Arizona, and the southern portions of Utah and Colorado. The largest Anasazi villages were concentrated in the region known today as the Four Corners, where the states of Arizona, New Mexico, Utah, and Colorado meet. Well-known ruins of Anasazi settlements include those of Canyon de Chelly and Kayenta in Arizona, Mesa Verde in Colorado, and Chaco Canyon in New Mexico. While the Zunis' ancestors were on the periphery of Anasazi territory, they had contact with and were influenced by a number of Anasazi settlements, especially the one at Chaco Canyon.

Early in the Anasazi period, around A.D. 1100 or 1200, a Zuni settlement called the Village of the Great Kivas was built. The village contained three large masonry structures, varying in size from six to sixty rooms, all built at ground level, as well as nine round ceremonial kivas, seven of which were about the size of a single house. The remaining two kivas were much larger, measuring fifty-one and seventy-eight feet in diameter, and were built in front of the village. These great kivas have benches attached to their interior walls, presumably used for seating during rituals, and also contain two vaults beneath the main floor.

During the Anasazi period, the Zunis' ancestors built several villages in valleys along the Zuni River and its tributaries. Some of these settlements were situated near cliffs that gave residents protection from wind and snowstorms. By the thirteenth century, the Zunis' ancestors began to construct villages on top of mesas, giving the inhabitants a clear view of all approaches to the village and making defense of the village easier. One such village is Atsinna, located on a mesa known as Inscription Rock. The entire village of Atsinna formed a rectangle, measuring 215 by 300 feet; its approximately 1,000 rooms were joined together in housing clusters. Some of the houses had only ground-floor rooms, while others had rooms on a second and third floor as well. The houses at Atsinna all faced inward, opening onto a large inner plaza.

Sometime in the fourteenth century Anasazi people in the Four Corners region suddenly abandoned their large towns and settled in smaller villages. The reason for this move is not certain, but most modern researchers suggest that a drastic climatic change, most probably a series of lengthy droughts, impelled the move. Some of the Anasazi people then established villages along the Rio Grande in New Mexico, using water from the large river to irrigate their farms. Other people, including the Zunis and the nearby Hopis, remained away from the Rio Grande in the dry desert lands of New Mexico and Arizona.

Although the Zunis did not move to the Rio Grande, during this period many people did move from towns located in the eastern half of Zuni territory into towns located farther west. The six Zuni villages discovered by the Spanish conquistadores in the sixteenth century—Halona ("red ant place" and the home of the itiwana), Hawikuh, Kiakima ("house of eagles"), Matsaki, Kwakina ("town of the entrance place"), and Kechipauan ("gypsum place")—were established as a result of this migration.

Local and regional trade was an important feature of life in the American Southwest. The Zunis traded directly with their

Shown here is Acoma Pueblo, or "sky city," which sits atop a 357-foot sandstone mesa in northwestern New Mexico. The term *Zuni* was adopted by the Spanish and comes from a Keresan language, which was spoken by the Acoma Pueblos.

neighbors and, through trade networks, with Native Americans living in other areas. As early as A.D. 600–900 the Zunis' ancestors had trade relations with peoples in Mexico, California, and the Great Plains. By A.D. 1250 Zuni villages, especially Hawikuh, had become centers for intertribal trade and were visited by peoples from throughout the American Southwest and adjacent regions. The Zunis traded corn, salt taken from Zuni Salt Lake (located approximately sixty miles south of Halona), turquoise from local mines, and buffalo hides obtained by Zuni hunters on expeditions into the Great Plains, as well as cotton cloth, jewelry, baskets, pottery, moccasins, and a distinctive blue paint. In return the Zunis received pottery, copper, and parrot feathers from Mexico; buffalo hides from the Great Plains; and seashells and coral from California.

The Zunis maintained peaceful relations with most of their neighbors in the Southwest. Many of these peoples, including the Hopis, Tewas, Tanos, and Keres, were culturally similar to the Zunis; consequently, these groups are often grouped together as the Pueblo Indians. Although Pueblo Indians share many cultural features, they are distinct peoples and speak different languages—indeed, the Pueblo languages come from several entirely separate linguistic families, and Zuni is different from all other languages spoken in the region. Linguists today are uncertain as to whether Zuni is a language isolate, with no known connections to any other language, or whether it belongs to a language family called Penutian, in which case it is a remote relative of languages spoken in parts of California. The language of the nearby Hopis belongs to a family called Uto-Aztecan, distantly related to the language spoken by Aztecs in Mexico. The Pueblo Indians who live along the Rio Grande speak languages belonging to two other language families, Tanoan and Keresan. One result of the different languages used among the Pueblo Indians is that the Zunis are not called by the name they call themselves, the *A:shiwi* (pronounced with a long *a*). *Zuni* comes from a word in a Keresan language used by the Acoma Pueblos to refer to the A:shiwis; it was picked up by the Spanish from the Acomas and has since come into general use.

By the time the Spanish arrived to misname them, the Zunis had long established a stable, peaceful, and prosperous way of life in the itiwana of the world. Not only had they managed to develop the material resources of their relatively harsh surroundings, but they had also created a complex society intimately linked with their natural environment.

2

The Zunis and the Raw People

For the people of the itiwana, religion was the center of life, giving meaning to all activities. Success in farming, childbirth, and many other aspects of life was considered to be due to the aid of the *Raw People*, the Zuni name for the many powerful deities and spirits in Zuni religion. These spirits were called Raw People because they ate raw foods as well as the cooked foods given to them as offerings by humans, who were called the Cooked People or Daylight People. In addition to making offerings, humans expressed respect and gratitude to the Raw People by saying prayers and performing rituals in their honor. In exchange, Raw People protected humans and gave them long lives, healthy children, personal courage, bountiful crops, successful hunts, and good fortune.

The many kinds of Raw People were associated with various natural forces or entities. Some Raw People were believed to be the spirits of animals, birds, or objects such as the sun, earth, and celestial bodies. Three very powerful Raw People were Earth Mother, Sun Father, and Moonlight-Giving Mother. Earth Mother was the place of life's origin, while Sun Father and Moonlight-Giving Mother gave humans light and good fortune (they were

The Zuni Universe

According to Zuni beliefs, the earth is surrounded by an ocean inhabited by four giant feathered serpents of the colors yellow, blue, red, and white. Along the shores of the ocean live "Rain Priests" of the six directions (north, west, south, east, the zenith, and the nadir) who become clouds, rain storms, fog, and dew when they leave their usual habitats. The Rain Priests are assisted by six "Bow Priests," who are the makers of thunder and lightning.

The Zunis believe that the world is divided into six directions, each one associated with various colors, animals, birds, and trees. This system of linkages underscores a basic principle of Zuni philosophy, namely that all life is interconnected and unified by a spiritual order. The associations of directions, colors, and animal forms provide basic symbolism of this unity. The associations include:

Direction	Color	Prey Animal	Game Animal
North	Yellow	Mountain Lion	Mule Deer
West	Blue	Bear	Mountain Sheep
South	Red	Badger	Antelope
East	White	Wolf	Whitetail Deer
Zenith	All Colors	Eagle	Jackrabbit
Nadir	Black	Mole	Cottontail Rabbit

Direction	Bird	Tree
North	Oriole	Pine
West	Bluejay	Douglas Fir
South	Parrot	Aspen
East	Magpie	Cottonwood
Zenith	Purple Martin	
Nadir	Swallow	

also husband and wife). Sun Father was considered especially important because he was the source of daylight, which was considered tantamount to life by the Zunis; indeed, the word for "daylight" and the word for "life" are the same in the Zuni

Every Zuni household keeps a sacred bundle that contains spiritually powerful objects and substances representing eternal natural and spiritual forces and the bounty of the universe. These bundles include water, plant seeds, stone carved images of animals, and ceremonial masks. They are reminders of the sacred relationship between Zunis and the deities, or Raw People, who guard and protect the people. Zunis show their respect for the spirits and give thanks to them by making offerings of tobacco smoke, small portions of cooked food, and cornmeal that may be mixed with crushed jewels, such as turquoise, shell, and coral. People also sacrifice wooden prayer sticks that are painted, carved with faces, and decorated with feathers. Since the sticks represent or stand in for the person making the sacrifice, the supplicant is essentially sacrificing a surrogate of him/herself. Special sacrifices are made by women to Moonlight-giving Mother while men give to Sun Father. Everyone makes sacrifices to the ancestors, a generalized class of spirits. Offerings are always given at the times of the summer and winter solstices, marking the changes in seasons and the earth's cycles. People may make offerings at many other times throughout the year as well, if they are moved to do so.

Zunis conceive of life as a path or road that is given to each person by Sun Father at his/her birth. The length of the road corresponds to the years that a person will live. Therefore, everyone hopes to be able to live out their apportioned path, trying to avoid dying before their time. Early deaths are usually thought to be caused by carelessness, accident, or witchcraft.[*]

* Adapted from Edward Dozier, *Pueblo Indians of North America* (New York: Holt, Rinehart and Winston, 1970), 205–206.

language. Because of Sun Father's special role, sunrise was considered the most sacred time of day.

Other Raw People were associated with directions or with specific locations, such as lakes and mountains. According to Zuni cosmology, the world is oriented to six sacred directions: north, east, south, west, above (the zenith), and below (the nadir). In addition to these directions, there is the itiwana, or middle, that connects the various elements of the universe. Directions in space help to set the boundaries of the world and to orient individuals to their places in it. Each direction is associated with certain colors, animals, birds, and trees. For the Zunis, this system of linkages underscored the spiritual unity and interconnection of all life in the universe.

The various elements of the world were kept alive and in balance by the efforts of the Raw People. In return for their protection and benevolence, the Zunis gave the Raw People food such as cornmeal (sometimes mixed with crushed turquoise, shell, or coral), tobacco smoke, and small portions of cooked food. They also offered the deities sacred ceremonial sticks, called prayer sticks, that the men would make from the wood of willow trees by carving faces into a piece of wood and decorating it with paint and feathers. Although only men could make the sticks, both women and men offered them to spirits or ancestors. The offering of prayer sticks formed an important part of many ceremonies, especially those marking the summer and winter solstices (June 21 and December 21).

In addition to honoring the Raw People, Zuni rituals were used to mark various critical stages in people's lives, including birth, puberty, marriage, and death. When a baby was born, its female relatives performed a variety of important duties. The baby's maternal grandmother would assist her daughter in the birth, but once the baby was born its paternal grandmother would come to the home and recite prayers asking the Raw People to protect the baby. She then would bathe the baby, rub ashes on its body, prepare a bed of warm sand for it to lie in, and remain with mother and child for eight days. At sunrise on the eighth day after birth, the paternal grandmother would wash the baby's head, place cornmeal in its hands, and then take the baby out into the dawn air, facing east toward the rising sun. While other female relatives sprinkled cornmeal toward the east, the grandmother would offer a prayer of blessing:

> Now this is the day.
> Our child,
> Into the daylight
> You will go standing.
> Now this day
> Our sun father,
> Having come out standing to his sacred place,
> Our child,
> It is your day.
> The flesh of the white corn,
> Prayer meal,
> To our sun father
> This prayer meal we offer.
> May your road be fulfilled
> Reaching to the road of your sun father.

This prayer reflected a number of Zuni beliefs. The Zunis thought of life as a road that every individual follows according to his or her own destiny. Sun Father assigned a specific road to each newborn baby, and all people hoped to live until they reached the proper end of their roads. Accidents or evil beings could interfere, however, and cause a premature death. Consequently a newborn's grandmother prayed that her grandchild would be protected and allowed to live out his or her appointed road. The paternal grandmother also chose the baby's name, but babies were not named immediately after birth. Instead, the family would wait until they were sure that

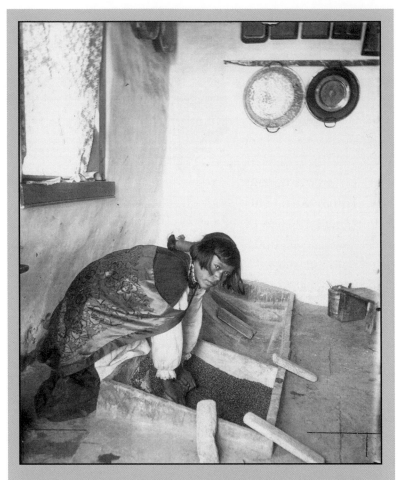

Corn was sacred to the Zunis and it was often ground into meal inside *metates*, which were specialized grinding stones. Grinding corn was an important ritual ceremony for girls who were entering puberty, because it represented one of the primary duties for Zuni women.

the infant was a healthy one and was likely to survive. Usually the name given the baby was the same as that of a relative on either side of the family who had lived a long life.

When a young Zuni girl reached puberty, another important set of rituals would take place. The adolescent girl would go to the home of her paternal grandmother, where she would spend a full day grinding corn—an act significant on both a secular and religious level. Grinding corn into meal was one of the primary duties of Zuni women, so in completing this ritual the girl would perform the practical work expected of adult women. Corn was also considered a sacred plant by the Zunis, a gift brought to them by six Raw People known as the Corn Maidens. Corn was believed to be the literal flesh of these powerful Raw People and to have great spiritual power; consequently, it was used in practically every religious ceremony—and only women could keep, prepare, and distribute this essential substance. The performance of the corn-grinding ceremony thus indicated that a girl was now old enough to take on the important religious responsibilities of adult Zuni women, as well as their secular duties.

After a young lady reached puberty, she was expected to become a wife. After a man and woman decided that they wanted to marry, the woman would consult with her mother to make sure that the union met with the family's approval. Then for several weeks the couple would attempt a trial marriage. The man would come to the woman's home at night, stay with her, and leave before dawn. During this time either the man or the woman could choose not to marry. If the woman decided against marriage, the matter ended immediately, but if the man changed his mind, he had to give the woman a gift before the bond was broken.

In most cases the couple would continue their relationship and become officially married. The Zuni marriage ceremony was fairly simple, and was both performed and celebrated by various exchanges of gifts. Female relatives of the woman and man involved would give each other presents of food, clothing, and jewelry. As part of this ceremonial exchange of gifts, the woman would grind a large supply of corn to present to her mother-in-law. The mother-in-law would accept the cornmeal and give the bride a set of festive clothing. The couple would then return to the bride's home. The next morning the husband would leave after sunrise and return in the early evening to share dinner with his new family. At this point, the couple would be considered husband and wife by the community.

The marriage ceremony could be further streamlined if a man decided to propose marriage without prior consultation or discussion. In this case, the man would simply bring a number of gifts to the woman's house and place them in the center of the room. The woman's father would then ask him to explain his intentions. The man would state his desire for marriage, and the father would respond by saying, "It is up to my daughter." At that point, the woman could accept or reject the proposal.

Death among the Zunis marked a time of sorrow and solemn ritual, in contrast to the informality of marriage rites. The deceased person's paternal aunt would come to the home and bathe the body in suds made from a yucca plant. She would then rub cornmeal on the body and dress it in new clothes, making a gash in each garment so that spirits of the clothes could accompany the person's soul on its journey to the after-world. Relatives would come to the deceased's home and express their grief through words and tears, and the deceased's brothers would dig a grave and carry the body out for burial. The body was placed in the grave so that the head faced east, the direction of the rising sun. A number of the deceased's pos-sessions were placed in the grave for the soul's use in the after-world, while the rest of the deceased's personal belongings were later burned or buried in a separate spot.

After the burial, a four-day period of intense mourning was observed by the surviving spouse. The spouse had to stay away from fire, bathe only in cold water, avoid meat and salt, remain quiet, and keep away from others as much as possible. Most Zuni couples resided with the wife's relatives; consequently, if a wife died, the surviving husband had to leave the house and return permanently to his mother's or sister's home—a prac-tice reflected in a Zuni saying, "Death takes two, not one." The saying also reflected the belief that during the four days of mourning the deceased's soul might try to take a companion, such as a close family member, along on the journey to the afterworld. During this period, the soul stayed in the village and sometimes made itself known to the living by scratching on surfaces, opening and closing doors, or appearing in dreams.

At the end of the four days, the soul would leave the village of the living and travel west to the village where souls reside. This village was located at the bottom of a sacred lake, two days' journey from the town of Zuni. If death was premature, however, the soul could not reach its final destination immediately but had to wait at a spot called Spirit Place, located one mile west of Zuni, until the time it should have reached the end of the road given to it at birth by Sun Father. When its appointed end finally came, the waiting soul could join its companions in the village under the lake.

The Zunis believed that the living and dead were eternally linked. The living had to honor the spirits of deceased ancestors, family members, and even enemy soldiers with prayers, food, and rituals performed for their pleasure. In return, the spirits would protect the living from harm and, if properly honored, would even transform themselves into rain clouds and bless the living with valuable rainfall.

The living and the dead were connected in yet another way, through the *kachina* impersonators. According to Zuni myth, during the tribe's wandering before finding the itiwana some children were killed beside a lake. The itiwana was found, but the parents of the children missed them terribly and were always sad. To cheer them up, the spirits of the children (who had formed the village of souls underneath the lake) came to visit, bringing blessings and rainfall. These were the first kachinas (*kokko* in Zuni). Although their visits brought the Zunis much joy, every time the kachinas returned to the village of the dead, they took the soul of a living person with them. The Zunis finally discussed this problem with the kachinas, who decided that they would no longer visit the Zunis in person but

would only visit as rainfall. So that they might still enjoy dancing for the living, they allowed the Zunis to impersonate them
by dressing in their costumes and masks and mimicking their
dances and behavior.

Impersonating a kachina was no ordinary task. Kachinas
had great magical power and in a sense possessed their impersonators. The masks and costumes used by kachina impersonators were made and handled with a great deal of care and
religious ceremony; they were considered both sacred and alive
and perfectly capable of harming or killing a disrespectful or
sinful impersonator. In addition, kachina impersonators had to
perform intricate and lengthy public dances to properly honor
the kachinas; these dances required days of rehearsal and sometimes lasted for hours. Creative Zunis could discover new
kachinas to impersonate or invent new dances to perform, provided that they were considered appropriate by religious leaders, but the older forms were always considered more powerful
and holier.

In order to maintain the kachina tradition, six specialized
ritual groups called kachina societies emerged among the
Zunis. All Zuni men were members of one of the six Zuni
kachina societies, which performed dances four times every
year—just before the winter solstice, later in winter, in summer, and at harvesttime. On these days, the dancers would don
their masks and costumes and enter the village at dawn. Led by
their kachina chief and watched by almost everyone in the village, the dancers would perform in the town's public plazas.
While kachina dances obviously had great religious significance, they were also loved because of their beauty. Indeed,
one of the expressed purposes of the kachina dances was to
provide entertainment for the village, and audience members
could request that a particularly good dance be repeated again
and again.

Kachina societies also held ceremonies in kivas. Each of the
six kivas in Zuni was associated with a specific kachina society.

Zuni kivas were special square-shaped rooms that were entered and exited by a ladder that extended through an opening in the ceiling; inside were large open spaces where dances and rituals were performed, with benches built against the walls to provide seating. In addition, kivas contained smaller rooms where highly secret rituals were conducted.

Zuni boys were inducted into kachina societies by their ceremonial fathers, a kind of godfather chosen by the boy's parents. A ceremonial father would induct his godson into his own kachina society when the boy was about five or six years old. During this initiation ceremony, the boy was washed by the wife of his ceremonial father, then carried by the ceremonial father to his kiva. Several boys were inducted at once, and when they all arrived at the kiva, adult members of the kachina society would enter dressed as kachinas and whip the boys to purify them. Although the whipping itself was usually quite gentle and painless, the experience was nonetheless an intimidating one for the boys, because at this point they usually did not know that the kachinas were human impersonators. When the whipping ended, the ceremonial fathers would take the purified children home.

When the purified boys reached about ten or twelve years of age, the second stage of initiation into the kachina societies occurred. The boys were again taken by their ceremonial fathers to the kivas and were whipped (usually more severely than during the initial purification) by the kachinas. This time, when the whipping ended, the impersonators would remove their masks, revealing to the boys that they were indeed human beings. The two groups then reversed roles, with the boys putting on the masks and whipping the adults. In this way, the boys gained the knowledge necessary for them to carry on the kachina society rituals.

The kachina societies were only six of the many Zuni religious societies. Each year, twelve Zuni men were chosen to impersonate six deities known as the *Shalakos*. The Shalakos

The Shalako festival is held every year by the Zunis in the late fall in the hopes of bringing abundant crops and many children. During the ceremony, twelve Zuni men impersonate six deities known as the Shalakos. This 1896 photo shows two Shalakos performing during the festival at Zuni Pueblo.

were powerful, birdlike beings who performed dances in new homes built especially for them every year in the late fall and brought good fortune, abundant crops, and many children. Shalako impersonators wore especially distinctive masks and costumes that made them over ten feet tall.

Another special group of masked gods was made up of ten ritual clowns called the Mudheads or *Koyemshis*. Unlike the Shalakos, the Koyemshis appeared in numerous dances and public rituals throughout the year, and different people could imitate a particular Koyemshi at different events. According to Zuni myth, the Koyemshis were the result of a sexual liaison between a brother and sister and, because of this incest, were both idiotic and impotent. Koyemshi impersonators wore mud-colored masks with foolish-looking faces and a short kilt of black cloth. Instead of wearing underclothes, Koyemshi impersonators had their penises tied down with cotton cord to symbolize both the childishness and the infertility of the Koyemshis. Each Koyemshi had a distinct personality; for example, one Koyemshi was a terrific coward, one was incredibly afraid of shadows and dark things, and one mistakenly believed that he was invisible. Koyemshi impersonators engaged in comical, outrageous, and often obscene behavior; exposing themselves, shouting obscenities, and making fun of spectators, kachina dancers, and priests.

Despite their foolish and unacceptable behavior (which also served as an example of how not to act), the Koyemshis were revered by the Zunis. They were believed to be Raw People of great antiquity, predating even the kachinas, and consequently were considered to have great power to bring fortune and rain. The Koyemshis' great power also made them potentially dangerous. At a certain point in the year, the Zunis were expected to give gifts to the Koyemshi impersonators. To begrudge the Koyemshis anything at this time, even in thought, was considered an invitation to disaster.

Another type of ritual clown was the *Neweekwe*. While they often appeared at the same events as the Koyemshis, the Neweekwes were not impersonators of Raw People but were instead members of perhaps the most remarkable of the many Zuni medicine societies. All of these societies performed dances and rituals intended to cure illness, but the Neweekwe were the only such society to engage in ritual clowning. Like the Koyemshi impersonators, members of the Neweekwe Medicine Society often behaved in a wild or obscene manner, but unlike the Koyemshi, they were not expected to take on specific personas. Consequently, the Neweekwes often engaged in far more sophisticated forms of clowning than the childish Koyemshis, including sometimes-biting parodies of current events. Since the Neweekwe Medicine Society specialized in curing stomach ailments, Neweekwe clowns would demonstrate the strength of their stomachs by drinking undrinkable fluids, such as urine, and eating inedible things, such as ashes, pebbles, wood chips, and feces.

While most Zuni medicine societies did not go to the extremes of the Neweekwes in demonstrating their effectiveness, members of some medicine societies did engage in especially dramatic displays of their skills. Healers belonging to the Snake Medicine Society and the Little Fire Society bathed in fire, swallowed fire, and danced on hot coals without getting burned. Members of the Sword People bathed in icy water in the wintertime and swallowed swords and sticks without getting cut. These spectacular public rituals not only displayed the powers of the various medicine societies but were also believed to bring good health to the community in general. Both men and women could learn to perform these rituals by volunteering to join a medicine society. In addition to learning a society's signature dramatic exploit, members of a medicine society learned the healing properties of roots, plants, massages, and rituals. Although some medicine societies relied more on medical cures and others more on ritual ones, every medicine society had its specialty and would treat patients whenever their services were needed—although a patient who had received successful medical treatment from a society was often compelled to join that society.

The Zunis, like all peoples throughout the world, had a complex theory of causes and treatments of disease. Most ailments were believed to have a spiritual or supernatural cause; consequently, it was believed necessary to accurately diagnose the spiritual cause and treat it through religious ritual rather than simply eliminating obvious symptoms. Although there were many potential reasons for illness, most ailments were believed to result from the actions of spirits or witches. Spirits could harm someone who had violated ritual rules or had not properly honored deities and ancestors. Witches—spiteful, jealous, and malicious humans with magical knowledge—would cause harm in retaliation for a slight or out of envy for another's good fortune.

Spirits and witches often caused illness by magically shooting a foreign object, such as a pebble, a piece of wood, or a feather, into their victims. The harmful object had to be found and extracted for the patient to recover. Certain healers were able to see into a patient's body, locate the hidden object, and draw it to the surface either with an eagle feather or by sucking on the body. These healers gained their knowledge from the spirit of the bear, the most powerful of animal patrons.

Witches could also cause illness by reciting harmful spells over objects that used to belong to the intended victim, such as nail clippings, bits of hair, or pieces of clothing. Such spells could cause the victim to sicken or die. In this situation, a healer would attempt to break the spell through prayers and rituals. If the healer or patient knew the identity of the witch, the patient's family could try to convince or force the witch into confessing and removing the spell.

Yet another important group of religious societies consisted of priesthoods. The most powerful was the *Rain Priesthood*—not surprisingly, given the importance of rain to the Zunis' survival. The Rain Priests were all men of high moral character; they avoided spiritually polluting arguments and conflicts and derived their knowledge and powers from the Rain-Bringing Spirits, who were among the most honored of deities.

One of the primary duties of the Rain Priests was to go on retreats to pray and perform rituals that would bring rain to the Zunis. Some of the rituals involved sacred bundles, which contained holy objects of great power, such as corn, cornmeal, seeds, feathers, prayer sticks, and stone effigies of spirit animals. The Rain Priesthood was made up of small groups of priests who would conduct four- or eight-day retreats in succession throughout the year, so that the community would never be without their spiritual aid.

Another prestigious group was the *Bow Priesthood*, which was believed to have obtained its power from the twin War

Gods who led the Zunis out of the earth in ancient times. Membership in the Bow Priesthood was required for warriors who had killed an enemy in combat; by joining the priesthood, the warrior obtained protection against the spirit of his deceased enemy, who would otherwise seek revenge. The responsibilities of the Bow Priesthood were both more secular and more martial than those of the Rain Priesthood. Bow Priests were responsible for carrying out warfare and keeping order in the villages; guarding the many trails that the Zunis used to conduct local, regional, and long-distance trade; and carrying out the decisions made by the Zunis' ruling council of religious leaders, which consisted of the heads of various religious orders, including the Rain Priesthoods, kachina societies, and medicine societies. Bow Priests also conducted the trials of people accused of witchcraft and performed the execution of unrepentant witches. (It should be noted that in Zuni society the crime of witchcraft legally encompassed not only the casting of evil spells but also a variety of less magical criminal acts, including murder.)

The common religious beliefs and practices of the Zunis helped keep their community strong and united. Private and public ceremonies were a focus of people's activity all year long, and anyone who was not planning, rehearsing, or conducting religious rituals at any given time participated as an audience member. Zuni religious societies also reduced factionalism within the community by splitting their members' allegiances between their family, or *clan*, and the religious society or societies to which they belonged. Consequently, disagreements between clans or religious societies almost never posed a serious threat to the basic unity and stability of the Zuni community.

3

Community Life

The people of the itiwana made good use of their land. For thousands of years they grew crops, gathered wild plants, and hunted animals. They established small communities, developing strategies that enabled them to thrive in the sometimes harsh environment of the American Southwest.

The Zunis almost always divided work along gender lines. While the Zunis believed that men and women were suited for different tasks, they also believed that gender was more of an acquired than an innate state. Consequently, men who so wished could live as women, wearing women's clothes, performing work traditionally assigned to women, and even taking other men as husbands. Such people were called *lhamana* by the Zunis and were considered a gender distinct from males or females. Family members would sometimes encourage young boys who showed an interest in women's work or in behaving like women to become lhamanas (women in the family were often

Zunis believed that gender was an acquired rather than an innate state; thus men could live like women if they chose. Known as lhamanas, these Zunis were not discriminated against. Perhaps the most famous lhamana was We-Wha (shown here), who visited Washington, D.C., in 1886.

especially encouraging; lhamanas were considered hard workers and a tremendous help around the house), but the final decision was made by the boy himself when he reached puberty. After a boy decided to become a lhamana, his religious education would continue as though he were a man, but his vocational education would be entirely that of a woman. The lhamana tradition eventually died out in the twentieth century due to the rabid opposition of U.S. authorities to the practice.

The work of Zuni men centered on the production of food, and they prepared the land, planted seeds, and harvested crops. Some of these tasks were carried out by individuals, while other work, such as the preparation of fields for planting and the harvesting of crops, was done collectively, usually by a group of relatives.

But the primary difficulty for Zuni farmers was not labor but the water supply. The climate in the Southwest is generally dry, with rainfall averaging only ten to fifteen inches per year. The rain that does fall comes in sudden and severe storms in summer months, which can drown or wash away young plants. The only other natural sources of water in the region are the small Zuni River and a few springs. To make the best use of available water, the Zuni farmers developed a system of flood-water irrigation, which involved building small dams and canals with mud walls to direct water from rainfall and over-flowing streams to the crops. This method was quite successful, and the Zunis cultivated as many as ten thousand acres of corn, producing a large enough surplus in good years to keep a two-year supply on hand in case of losses from drought or damage caused by insects.

In addition to farming, Zuni men hunted in the surround-ing plains, deserts, and mountains. Hunting was usually done in groups, sometimes as large as one hundred or two hundred people. Closer to the villages small animals, such as rabbits, mice, and other desert rodents, were found in abundance, while the more distant woodlands and mountains contained large animals, such as deer, antelope, elk, mountain sheep, and bears. Zuni men hunted rabbits with sticks thrown like boomerangs and hunted deer by driving them either into fenced enclosures or into pits dug in the ground, where they could easily be killed.

Zuni men also fished in the Zuni River and its tributaries and snared birds, using delicate traps of wood and twine designed specifically for each species. They trapped eagles, ducks, wild turkeys, hawks, owls, crows, and blue jays, using their flesh for food and their feathers for decorating clothing and ceremonial equipment. In addition to the trapped wild birds, Zuni families kept flocks of domesticated turkeys, which were tended by all household members. These turkeys were raised mainly for their feathers, but when other food was scarce they were also eaten.

Zuni women were responsible for preparing, cooking, and preserving foods. One of their most time-consuming tasks was grinding corn. Many Zuni breads and cakes were made of

Zuni Corn ("a'ta'a" or "the seed of seeds")

Although Zuni men planted a variety of crops, corn was given the most attention both in terms of human activity and ceremonial care. Farmers kept a store of seeds taken from all six varieties of corn (white, yellow, blue, red, black, and speckled), representing the most perfect ears grown in the previous harvest. The seeds were kept in a family "corn room" or "granary." They were prayed over when put away for storage and again when taken out for planting. In the description of anthropologist Frank Cushing, who lived with the Zunis in the 1880s:

> The farmer next chose six kernels of corn, one of each of the different colors, proclaiming to the women there, "We go!" And, as he steps out of the doorway, "the corn matron hustles after him with a bowl of fresh, cold water, with which she lavishly sprinkles him, laughingly telling "them" to go. Thoroughly bedrenched, he shuffles down the hill, across the river, and out to his field.[*]

The seeds were sprinkled over in order to symbolize the rain needed to nourish them and help them grow. The farmer then planted the first seeds into small holes in the ground, covered the grains and returned home, remaining away from the fields for four days, during which time he fasted and prayed at sunrise. When he finally returned to the fields, he buried the seeds into small holes dug from four to seven inches into the earth, putting some fifteen to twenty kernels in each in order to assure that at least some would yield plants.

Corn was harvested by groups of related men working together. They were usually either fathers and sons, brothers, cousins, or in-laws. The men husked some of the corn immediately in the fields so that the husks could decay and cornmeal, and it took hours of careful work to produce an adequate amount. Different recipes called for different consistencies of corn meal, ranging from coarse to very fine, and nuts and seeds were ground for food as well. As a result, a Zuni woman owned several grinding stones with varying edges to

fertilize the earth but most were taken back to the village where they were husked and dried by groups of women. A large supply was kept in sealed storage rooms as a surplus to be used in years of poor harvests.

Corn was ground into cornmeal and made into a great variety of recipes. Indeed, grinding corn was one of the most time-consuming tasks of Zuni women, requiring many hours of work to produce the large quantity of meal needed for breads and cakes. Grinding stones have different types of edges, together making meal of varying consistencies. Traditional corn dishes, many still prepared today, are either cooked in large pots of boiling water, on flat stones in open fireplaces within homes, or inside the dome-shaped ovens built outdoors on terraces. Boiled breads or dumplings are made from small balls of fine and coarse cornmeal and salt. After they are boiled in water, they harden and become somewhat pasty. Yellow cornmeal, sweetened with dried flowers, is made into a kind of pudding. The batter is then wrapped in green corn leaves and boiled or baked. Some types of corn bread are prepared with the addition of ashes or lime yeast used as a leavening.

After the flour is prepared, it is molded into thick cakes and cooked on hot coals or baked under hot ashes. The most prized corn bread is a delicacy called hewe, a paper-thin bread prepared on large baking stones. In order to make hewe, women grind all six varieties of corn into a fine flour that is then mixed with hot water to form a thin paste which is finally poured onto heated cooking stones. As soon as the batter is lightly toasted, it is peeled away from the stone. Hewe is eaten on ceremonial as well as domestic occasions and is given as gifts in ritual exchanges.

* Frank Cushing, *Zuni: Selected Writings of Frank Hamilton Cushing*, ed. Jesse Green (Lincoln, Nebr.: University of Nebraska Press, 1979), 261.

Zuni men and women often grew crops along the Zuni River, and they watered these crops by hand. In order to transport the water, Zuni women would pour the water in jars called *ollas* (shown here), which they would carry on their heads.

produce the different types of meal. Once the meal was ground, women would make it into batter to be either fried over a fire or baked in an oven.

Women as well as men grew crops but only in small gardens generally located along the banks of the Zuni River. These gardens, called waffle gardens because of their distinct appearance, were divided into small square or rectangular cells surrounded by low mud walls that helped to conserve water and protect the plants from wind. Women watered their gardens by hand, using ladles to distribute water that they carried from the Zuni River or from nearby wells. They brought water to gardens in jars called *ollas,* which they carried on their heads.

In addition to growing crops, women gathered many varieties of wild plants growing near their villages. Some of these plants were used for medicinal purposes, such as ointments for burns and eye irritations; painkillers for headaches, toothaches, and sore throats; salves to promote healing of wounds; and drugs to help women in childbirth. Other wild plants, such as nuts, watercress, yucca, juniper berries, sunflowers, wild rice, wild peas, wild potatoes, parsnips, and milkweed, were eaten as supplements to agricultural products and contributed valuable nutrients to people's diet. Because the Zunis relied on their corn and bean crops as their primary source of protein, nuts were especially important as an additional source of protein during crop failures.

Men and women each had specific duties when undertaking tasks such as building a house. The men built the outside structure of houses from sandstone blocks and slabs, then the women plastered the interior walls. The women were responsible for keeping up the plaster, applying fresh coats when the walls deteriorated over time. Women were also responsible for keeping a fire going to heat the houses in winter, but men were responsible for cutting and hauling home the firewood.

Zuni women and men also specialized in different crafts. Women were the potters and were responsible for all stages of the pottery-making process, from the digging of clay to the final painting. Men made the tools and gear used for farming and hunting, including digging sticks, shovels, axes, bows, and arrows. Men also produced a variety of household utensils and personal items. They made baskets from twined and coiled yucca and rabbitbrush, and they wove the cotton cloth that was fashioned into blankets, clothing, and sashes. Finally, men used turquoise (obtained from the Zunis' mines and quarries, which also produced silver, copper, and obsidian), shell, and coral to craft beautiful jewelry that was worn by all Zunis. Both men and women wore cotton garments and deerskin- or antelope-hide footwear. Women wore cotton blouses, skirts, and sashes, while men wore cotton shirts, sashes, and aprons over deerskin leggings. Cloth was often dyed with bright mineral or vegetable pigments, and clothing was decorated with embroidered geometric designs.

By skillfully developing their crafts and making good use of their resources, the Zunis lived in prosperity. Their comfortable and secure way of life was described in 1540 by Francisco Vasquez de Coronado, a Spanish officer who led an expedition through the Southwest:

> They have very good homes and good rooms with corridors and some quite good rooms underground and paved, built for the winter. The town of Granada [Coronado's name for the Zuni village Hawikuh] has two hundred houses, all surrounded by a wall. There is another town nearby, but somewhat larger than this, and another of the same size as this; the other four are somewhat smaller.
>
> The people of these towns seem to me to be fairly large and intelligent. They are well built and comely. I think that they have a quantity of turquoises.
>
> The food which they eat consists of maize, of which they have great abundance, beans, and game. They make the best tortillas that I have ever seen anywhere. They have the very best arrangement and method for grinding that was ever seen. They have very good salt in crystals, which they bring from a lake a day's journey distant from here.

The "very good homes" Coronado saw reflected the Zunis' family structure in their architecture. A Zuni house usually had one, two, or three stories of rooms arranged in rows, and related families would occupy a series of adjacent rooms. Zuni families were considered related through the women—married daughters remained in the household into which they were born, but married sons usually left home and moved into their wife's household. A traditional Zuni household included an extended family made up of an elder couple, their daughters, their daughters' husbands and children, and their unmarried sons. This structure weakened the authority of men in the household; consequently, the person who traditionally organized the activities of residents—and made sure that all necessary work was completed—in a Zuni household was the eldest woman. She was also the person to consult for advice concerning problems or major decisions.

In addition to the extended family, the Zunis' social system included kin groups called lineages. A lineage consists of people related by direct descent from a known ancestor or elder. Zuni lineages were *matrilineal,* or based on the principle of descent through women. The eldest surviving woman in a lineage was usually considered the head of that lineage and played an active role in the lives of its members by giving advice, settling disputes, and organizing group activities. In addition, the head woman would safeguard certain sacred objects that were considered the property of her lineage; these items were usually kept in a bundle placed on an altar erected in a special room of her house. The eldest brother of the head woman was also an important figure in a lineage and would also be consulted by lineage members faced with a conflict or an important decision.

These lineages were combined into larger kinship units called clans. A clan is a grouping of people who believe that they are related by descent from a common ancestor. A member of the more than a dozen Zuni clans could not always trace his or her specific familial relationship to every other member, but clan members believed they were all descendants of a specific figure of the ancient past. As with other Zuni kinship groups, Zuni clans were matrilineal, and Zuni children auto-matically belonged to the clan of their mother. Nonetheless, the Zunis also had close ties to their father's group, and individuals often referred to themselves as a "child of my father's clan." Clan membership strongly affected people's choice of a mar-riage partner. Since members of a clan were considered rela-tives, they could not marry each other. In addition, the Zunis condemned marriages between a person and someone in his or her father's clan.

In addition to their role in determining appropriate mar-riages, clans served several other functions in Zuni society. Each clan had control over certain areas of farmland within the Zuni territory. The elder women of a clan, who were the clan heads, distributed the land to the lineages and households within their group. Plots of farmland were controlled and could be inherited by the women of an individual household, but these plots were not truly private property belonging to individuals. Rather, land was considered a resource ultimately controlled by the clan as a whole, and members of the clan had the right to use the land according to their needs. Although the women of a household inherited the farmland, the men did the farmwork. A man would work on his mother's land until he married, at which time he would move into his wife's house-hold and work on her family's land.

Because Zuni relatives lived and worked together and shared food and other goods, family members tended to be deeply loyal and emotionally close to each other. Bonds between parents and sons and between sisters and brothers also remained strong even when a man left the household after marriage. Men were expected to frequently return to their first home to help celebrate family occasions and to give aid to their relatives. Indeed, if a man came from an important family that looked after especially sacred objects, he could easily spend more time with (and gain more status from) his own family than his wife's.

Zuni earthenware water jar, Colorado Historical Society, Denver, Colorado. Pottery such as this piece, which dates to the early twentieth century, was traditionally used for carrying water from the Zuni River to water crops.

Zuni prayer meal olla (bowl), Colorado Historical Society, Denver, Colorado. This bowl, circa 1870–1890, is decorated with dragonflies, frogs, and tadpoles.

Zuni buffed stone bear fetish, circa 1870–1890, Colorado Historical Society, Denver, Colorado. Fetishes hold great religious significance for Zunis and serve as messengers to assist the Zunis in their communications with their deities.

Zuni earthenware ceremonial bowl, Colorado Historical Society, Denver, Colorado. This late-nineteenth-century piece is decorated with a spotted frog, tadpoles, and dragonflies.

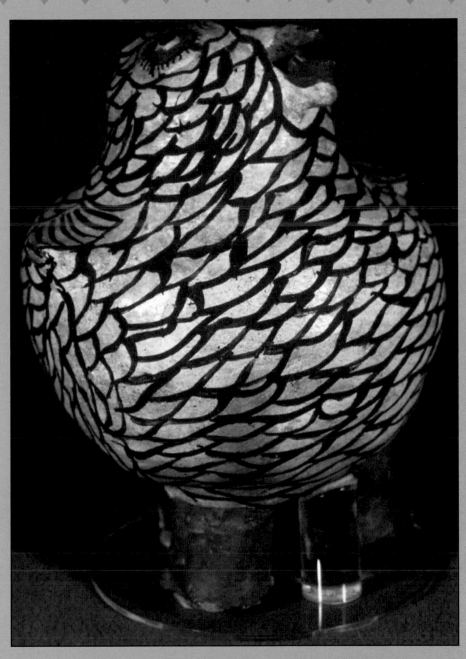

Zuni clay owl effigy, Colorado Historical Society, Denver, Colorado. Owls are often associated with witches in Zuni culture and parents told stories to their children warning them that they might be carried off by an owl if they misbehaved.

Zuni sand painting, Denver Public Library, Denver, Colorado. Sand paintings were often used in religious ceremonies and were created from dry pigments made from sandstone and crushed charcoal.

Zunis offered prayer sticks to deities during religious ceremonies, particularly those of the winter and summer solstices. The sticks were often made from the wood of willow trees and decorated with paint and feathers. These sticks from Zuni Pueblo are housed at the Ethnologisches Museum, Staatliche Museen zu Berlin, Germany.

Zuni water jar, Smithsonian Institution, National Museum of the American Indian, New York. The design on this jar represents the Zuni Rain Bird, which was thought to bring water to the parched lands of the Southwest.

The importance of kinship in Zuni life was reflected in people's way of addressing each other. Words used to address close relatives were also used to address other people in the clan. For example, Zunis would call elder women in their clan "mother" and older men in their clan "mother's brother"; older men in their father's clan would be addressed as "father" and older women in their father's clan as "father's sister"; and older people called their younger clanmates "daughter" or "son." The Zunis used kinship terms for close friends as well. For example, people who were close childhood friends would call each other "brother" or "sister" and each other's parents "mother" and "father." Even certain natural forms merited kinship terms; the earth was "mother" and the sun "father." Rain clouds and fire were called "grandmother," water "grandfather," and corn either "sister" or "brother."

The Zunis formed bonds with nonrelatives through marriage. Married couples were expected to act as partners, cooperating in their work and helping to support each other's families. Marriage was seen as a very personal activity, and conduct within a marriage was not regulated by any sort of law (although it could be rich fodder for gossip). Most marriages succeeded, but if a couple did not get along well, either spouse was free to divorce the other (although the woman kept any children). If the man chose to divorce, he simply left his wife's household and returned to his mother's home. If the woman wanted to end the marriage, she put her husband's belongings outside the house, and the man took his possessions and left. But when the marriage succeeded, the bonds it established extended beyond the couple to include both sets of relatives, and children born to the couple could depend upon the members of both their own household and their father's family (or, if their parents divorced, their stepfather's family) for support.

Child-rearing among the Zunis was not only the responsibility of the parent but also of the entire family. Grandparents were often especially indulgent of their grandchildren,

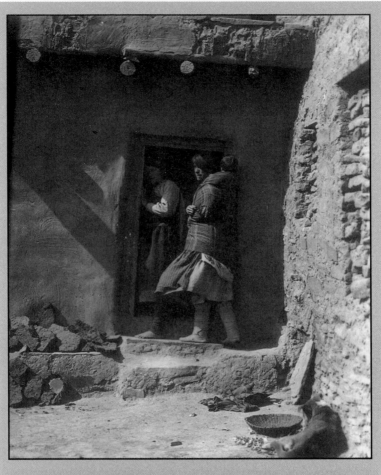

For the Zunis, child-rearing was the responsibility of the entire family. Shown here is a family entering their home at Zuni Pueblo.

instructing and entertaining them by recounting myths and histories of the people. To an extent, the entire community was engaged in the raising of each child, because any passer-by was considered free or even obligated to reprimand a misbehaving child. As Zuni children grew up, they gradually learned the tasks that would be required of them as adults. Boys would help their fathers in the fields by planting and weeding crops, while girls would learn to grind corn and would assist their mothers by tending to younger siblings. Zuni children were usually taught by example and encouragement, not by punishment; however, misbehaving children were sometimes told frightening stories about owls, witches, and certain kachinas who carried away naughty children. And if a mother was especially exasperated with her child, she would ask the chief of a kachina society to make sure one of the child-snatching kachinas was present at the next public dance. When the kachina appeared at the dance, it would approach the offending child and menace him, telling him that it was going to carry him off and eat him if he did not behave.

Ideally, Zuni girls and boys would grow up to be generous, helpful, considerate, and moderate people. These characteristics were strongly encouraged and valued by the community. Consequently, visitors to Zuni households were usually given a generous and hospitable welcome. According to Frank Cushing, a researcher who lived with the Zunis for many years in the late nineteenth century:

> The instant greeting to a Zuni house is "Enter, sit, and eat!" Enter any house at whatever time of day or night and the invariable tray of breads will be brought forth, also parched corn, or, if in the seasons, peaches, melons or piñon nuts.

The Zunis strongly disapproved of people who were boastful, argumentative, uncooperative, or stingy. According to Ruth Bunzel, an anthropologist who visited the Zunis from 1928 to 1933:

> In all social relations, whether within the family group or outside, the most honored personality traits are a pleasing address, a yielding disposition, and a generous heart. The person who thirsts for power, who wishes to be, as they scornfully phrase it, "a leader of the people," receives nothing but criticism.

Factionalism and public disagreements were discouraged. Disputes—even those involving fairly serious crimes—were supposed to be settled privately and quietly by the families of the people involved. If a person repeatedly acted in an unacceptable manner, the people in the community would make their disapproval obvious by publicly teasing the wrongdoer (this was often the duty of the ritual clowns) or gossiping about the person's actions to shame the wrongdoer into correcting his or her behavior. Repeated or serious misbehavior exposed a person to accusations of witchcraft, which could lead to ostracism from the tribe or, in extreme cases, execution.

The government of the Zunis consisted of a *pekwin*, who was the head secular authority, and a council of priests, who were responsible for managing collective work, community affairs, and religious ceremonies. Each village had its own pekwin and council. The pekwin was named to the position by a council of priests and could be removed from office by that same council if the people disapproved of his behavior. To become a pekwin, a man had to have a generous and kind disposition and to be respected by all; in addition, he had to be a member of the Dogwood clan. The pekwin was officially installed in office during a ceremony conducted by the head Rain Priest of the village, who would place a staff made of feathers in the chief's hands, recite a prayer, and then blow on the staff four times.

The council of priests appointed a pekwin to govern because it believed that if the priests became directly involved in village disputes, they would no longer be pure of heart, and their prayers would lose power. Priests nonetheless exercised a great deal of influence in the villages by setting moral examples and encouraging others to act properly. To help with the more practical problems of governance, the pekwin had two assistants who were warriors and members of the Bow Priesthood.

Thanks to a unique system of government, a thorough exploitation of the resources around them, and a social system that emphasized mutual support and cooperation, the Zunis created a smoothly functioning society that provided most individuals with lives of security and purpose. Even the Spanish conquistadores who came into Zuni territory in the mid-six-teenth century remarked on the orderliness and fellowship that marked Zuni society. One soldier, named Castaneda, wrote in 1540:

> They have priests who preach; these are aged men who ascend to the highest terrace of the village and deliver a ser-mon at sunrise. The people sit around and listen in profound silence. These old men give them advice in regard to their manner of living, which they think it their duty to observe; for there is no drunkenness among them, no unnatural vice; there are no thieves; on the contrary, they are very laborious.

The Zunis prospered through the centuries by developing their resources and living for the most part in harmony with the people around them. But their stability was threatened in the sixteenth century when invaders from Spain came into the American Southwest looking for treasures and remained there to dominate the original inhabitants.

4

Defending the Homeland

The Spanish invasion of the Southwest began in the middle years of the sixteenth century. The Spanish had defeated the rich Aztec Empire in central Mexico in 1521 and were seeking to extend their control over other, hopefully equally wealthy Native American tribes. Spanish explorers traveled through the northern provinces of Mexico, searching for cities filled with treasures, but they found only small groups of farmers, hunters, and gatherers. Eventually the explorers mounted expeditions into the territory of the Zuni and other Pueblo tribes. Accompanying these explorers were priests belonging to the Franciscan order of the Catholic Church, who hoped to convert the Native Americans to Christianity.

In 1538 the viceroy of Mexico, Antonio de Mendoza, chose a Franciscan priest named Fray Marcos de Niza to lead a party into present-day New Mexico and Arizona. The viceroy wanted to gain

Antonio de Mendoza was the first viceroy of New Spain, serving in that capacity from 1535 to 1550. Mendoza commissioned Francisco Vasquez de Coronado's expedition to New Mexico in the 1540s, in hopes of discovering the Seven Cities of Cibola, a mythical land of golden treasures.

subjects for the king of Spain and converts for the Catholic Church. He told Niza:

> You must explain to the natives of the land that there is only one God in heaven, and the Emperor on earth to rule and govern it, whose subjects they all must become and whom they must serve.

Marcos de Niza ventured into the American Southwest early in 1539, sending a small group in advance of the main contingent under the leadership of a Moor named Estevanico. Estevanico's party reached Zuni lands, but once they arrived, Estevanico gravely offended the tribe and was executed. Estevanico's specific offense is not known—according to Zuni oral tradition, the "black Mexican" was "greedy, voracious and bold"—but some have speculated that he unwisely informed the Zunis of the size and military nature of the larger party that was to join him.

In any case, when word of Estevanico's death reached Niza, he quickly returned to Mexico and told Viceroy Mendoza that he had found a kingdom richer even than the empire of the Aztecs. It is unclear whether Niza actually saw Hawikuh during his expedition; in any case, he wildly exaggerated its wealth, claiming that its houses were decorated with turquoise and other jewels. Niza also claimed that Hawikuh formed a part of a mighty empire called the Seven Cities of Cibola, and the territory of the Zunis was known as Cibola (probably a corruption of the Zuni phrase *Shi-wi-na*, used to indicate any permanent Zuni town or residence) and the Zunis themselves as Cibolans for years to come. Niza's fertile imagination was reflected in his name for the Cibolan Empire; the Zunis probably inhabited only six villages at this time, but both Aztec and European legend mentioned wealthy empires encompassing seven cities, so Niza credited the Zunis with seven.

Obviously, news of the Seven Cities of Cibola was quite welcome to Viceroy Mendoza, who sent a large force into the region to conquer the wealthy Cibolans and plunder their treasures. The expedition—consisting of 230 soldiers on horseback, 70 foot soldiers, several Franciscan priests, and hundreds of Mexican Indians—was led by Francisco Vasquez de Coronado. Coronado planned to force the Cibolans to submit to Spain's authority, while the Franciscans planned to establish missions and convert the empire of Cibola to Christianity.

The Zunis, of course, had their own plans. Expecting reprisals for the killing of Estevanico, the Zunis prepared for an attack at Hawikuh, evacuating all women, children, and elderly from the village onto nearby mesas. The Zunis made a preliminary attempt to drive off the Spanish by attacking them at a narrow canyon near the juncture of the Zuni and Little Colorado rivers, and they inflicted several casualties. But the Spanish continued toward Hawikuh, reaching an open plain south of town in early July 1540. According to a Spanish officer, when the Spanish arrived at the plain, they "found all the Indians of Cibola and the people of other places who had gathered to meet us with force."

Six hundred Zuni warriors were assembled to turn back the Spanish invasion. At first the battle went well for the Zunis, who managed to repel the initial Spanish assault, but the superior weaponry of the Spanish helped turn the tide, and when the soldiers began a second attack against Hawikuh, the Zunis, suffering serious casualties, surrendered the town. Coronado, who had been injured in the battle, and his men occupied Hawikuh. The village proved to be somewhat disappointing to the Spanish: Most of the residents had fled, and Hawikuh lacked the lavish riches reported by Niza. The conquistadores were quite impressed with the Zunis' agricultural bounty, but they were in search of gold, not grain, and eventually left Zuni territory to investigate the villages of the Pueblo tribes along the Rio Grande. Several priests and soldiers stayed behind for another two years to assert Spanish authority in the region; they returned to Mexico in 1542, leaving two Mexican Indian converts to Christianity to spread the word among the Zunis. According to a Spanish officer who was a member of the party traveling to Mexico, after they left Hawikuh, "For two or three days, the Zunis never ceased to follow the rear guard of the army to pick up any baggage or Indian servants . . . they rejoiced at keeping some of our people."

Although the party of priests and soldiers was harassed by

Zuni warriors, the two Mexican Indians left behind were treated quite well and, according to later visitors to Hawikuh, eventually recanted their Christianity and married into the tribe. This pattern was to be repeated throughout the period of Spanish conquest; the Zuni tradition of generosity and hospitality to strangers resulted in most visitors being treated quite well, but newcomers who attempted to disrupt or interfere with traditional Zuni life were threatened, harassed, or killed.

After Coronado left Zuni territory in 1540, he set up headquarters in the Pueblo village of Tiguex, located on the Rio Grande near present-day Bernalillo, New Mexico. From there he sent expeditions to contact and to obtain tribute from other Pueblo villages, eventually exercising dominion over nearly all the Rio Grande villages. The Zunis, however, were located far to the west of the Rio Grande, and after Coronado's disappointment the Spanish had little interest in exploiting their territory. As a result, for the next forty years the Zunis had no recorded contact with the Spanish, although informal meetings may have occurred, and the Zunis almost certainly obtained information on Spanish activities through their trade with the other Pueblo tribes.

In 1581 the Spanish, in an attempt to both enlarge their domain and investigate persistent rumors of incredible treasure to the west, sent an expedition into Zuni territory led by Francisco Sanchez Chamuscado, but the only riches he found were agricultural. Two years later, Antonio de Espejo led a contingent to the Zuni village of Matsaki, looking for copper and silver mines. He failed to find the mines and soon departed from the area, but he left behind several soldiers and priests in the area to codify Spanish control.

As with Coronado, the Zunis benefited immensely in their dealings with Espejo by being in an out-of-the-way location that was not believed to contain anything of great value. Espejo and his soldiers routinely demanded vast quantities of food and clothing from the Pueblo Indians who lived along the Rio

Grande, and they usually slaughtered the inhabitants of any village that defied them. Because of their location the Zunis escaped much of this mistreatment, but the combination of deference and defensive preparation that marked their future relations with the Spanish strongly indicates that they had heard tales of the repeated atrocities.

In 1598, the Spanish government established a permanent colony of settlers in what was called New Mexico and named Juan de Oñate as the first governor of the colony. Oñate was determined to exploit both the human and mineral resources of the colony, and he traveled to the territory of the Zunis in the year of his appointment to order the Zuni leaders to declare their obedience to the Spanish king and to explore their territory for valuable natural resources. Of special interest to Oñate were the rumored copper mines of the Zunis and Zuni Salt Lake, which could provide settlers with a popular seasoning and preservative. Oñate sent two parties of soldiers to explore and assess these potential sources of wealth. The soldiers sent to the mines reported that they had indeed found mines of great antiquity, but they were vague as to both the location and the potential value of the excavations. The soldiers sent to Zuni Salt Lake had more encouraging news, reporting that the lake had a crust of salt on it so thick that a man could walk on it and they brought back a sample of salt that Oñate declared superior to any found in Europe.

Oñate hardly left the area encouraged, however. As useful as a salt lake might be for supporting a settlement, it was hardly the literal gold mine he had hoped to find. Oñate's search for exploitable resources reached a head as complaints about his conduct led to threats that he would lose the governorship of New Mexico. He visited Zuni territory again in 1604, looking for the copper mines his men had supposedly located on the earlier expedition. A Spanish official who accompanied the expedition noted that four of the six Zuni villages were "almost completely in ruins," a fact that probably reflects the toll taken by European diseases, as well as the migrations caused by inter-mittent conflicts with passing Spanish soldiers.

Oñate's second search for the Zuni mines was a failure, and in 1607 authorities in Mexico removed him as governor of the colony and replaced him with Pedro de Peralta, who arrived in 1609 and established a provincial capital in the village of Santa Fe. Peralta, however, continued the abusive policies of his predeces-sors, exacting forced labor and tribute from the Rio Grande Pueblo Indians. The Franciscan missionaries also became quite powerful during this period and were equally brutal in their exploitation of the Native Americans. Missionaries forced the Pueblo Indians to work in their fields and homes, to build churches and houses in their villages, and to attend church ser-vices. In addition, many missionaries destroyed non-Christian ceremonial objects and religious works of art, and they pun-ished defiant or uncooperative Native Americans with public whippings, tortures, and executions. Native Americans who practiced their traditional religions were often viciously perse-cuted for practicing witchcraft, a crime defined by the Spanish as any exercise of non-Christian religious activities.

Once again the location of the Zunis' settlements allowed them to escape some of the more intense forms of control, but their experience with Spanish missionaries was negative enough that Spanish-speaking Catholics were banned from Zuni rituals and dances well into the twentieth century. The missionaries to the Zunis usually served a large area and never stayed long in any one village. As a result, the Zunis would usu-ally abstain from their public religious ceremonies when a mis-sionary was in town, then continue as usual once the missionary left.

The Zunis were no more cooperative with the secular Spanish authorities. The Zunis were expected to pay tribute and to perform work for Spanish authorities, including farmwork and the gathering of piñon nuts, which were sold by officials for huge profits in Mexico. But the Spanish soon discovered that the

Zunis would only pay tribute when threatened by an armed force, an expensive, tiresome, and not altogether safe way to make collections. Officials in Santa Fe eventually gave up on collecting tribute from the Zunis after 1621.

Eventually the Spanish tried to reassert control over the Zunis. In the late 1620s, an officer named Silva Nieto led a contingent of thirty soldiers and several priests into Zuni lands. Nieto demanded that the people submit to Spanish authority, but the Zunis, led by their council of religious elders, refused. Nieto departed but left two Franciscan priests to establish a mission in the village of Hawikuh. The presence of the priests was an immediate source of conflict, and Nieto had to return with his soldiers a few days after leaving to menace the Zunis into accepting them.

The priests—the first permanent resident missionaries in Zuni territory—were quick to begin what they considered the work of God. Using Zuni labor, they oversaw the construction of a mission compound in Hawikuh, which contained a massive church with a nave measuring 103 feet by 20 feet, as well as a kitchen, a chapel, residences, and workrooms. The compound was completed in 1632, and a second mission was established in the town of Halona at about the same time.

The Franciscan missionaries may have felt optimistic, but they had seriously underestimated the resentment caused by their use of Zuni labor and their interference with Zuni religious life. This resentment was worsened after a new priest—a blunt, opinionated, and unpopular man—arrived in Hawikuh determined to stamp out the Zunis' religion. Shortly after the compounds were built, the new priest attempted to interfere with a Zuni ceremony and force those in attendance to go to mass instead. The Zunis, infuriated at his audacity, killed him and another priest who was passing through the area and destroyed the missions. The other resident priests immediately vacated the territory, and officials in Santa Fe sent soldiers to punish the people responsible.

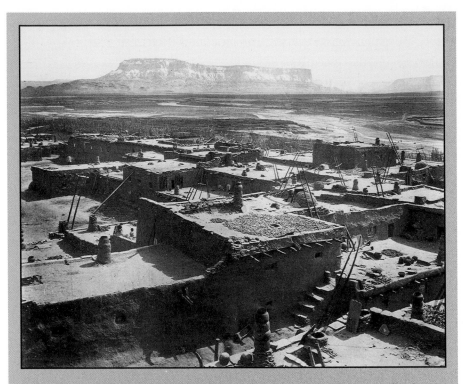

When the Spanish infiltrated Zuni territory in the early 1600s, the Zunis took refuge on Dowa Yallane, or Corn Mountain. Situated on the top of an easily defendable mesa, Dowa Yallane provided a safe haven for the Zunis and is one of the tribe's most sacred sites.

By the time the soldiers reached the Zuni villages, however, the Zunis had abandoned them and settled in a large community on top of an easily defendable mesa called Dowa Yallane, or Corn Mountain. The Zunis eventually allowed some missionaries accompanying the soldiers into their new village to negotiate a settlement. The Zunis promised to accept the authority of the Spanish crown, and the Spanish promised to allow the Zunis to return to their villages. The Spanish soldiers left the region, but the cautious Zunis remained on Dowa Yallane for another three years before returning to their old villages.

The lack of Spanish documentation concerning the Zunis from 1632 to 1680 seems to indicate that authorities made few additional attempts to control them at this time, although informal contact almost surely continued. A few missionaries took up residence in Zuni towns and attempted, with little success, to have the Zunis rebuild the missions. The missionaries did have some impact on Zuni life, however; when the Zunis publicly performed their traditional religious dances and ceremonies, the priests reportedly arrested a number of the religious leaders and punished them with public beatings, as well as by confiscating ritual objects and burning kivas. Despite what was surely bad blood between the missionaries and Zunis, only one missionary was reported as having been murdered during this period, and he was apparently the victim of Navajo or Apache raiders.

Resentment ran high against the Spanish nonetheless. In 1680, the Zunis joined a Pueblo Indian conspiracy, led by a Tewa named Pope, to oust the Spanish officials, soldiers, priests, and settlers from the Southwest. Pope and the other leaders planned a siege of the provincial capital of Santa Fe. They decided to start their rebellion in the summer, just before an annual delivery of supplies from Mexico, when the Spanish would have the fewest guns and ammunition. August 11, 1680, was set as the date for the rebellion, and two messengers were chosen to travel to all the towns and convey details of the planned uprising to all the Pueblo tribes. But the Spanish governor, Antonio de Otermin, found out about the impending revolt and arrested the two messengers on August 9. When word of the arrests spread in the villages, the leaders decided to begin the rebellion immediately. The Pueblo Revolt began on August 10, when the inhabitants of the Rio Grande villages cut off water and supplies to Santa Fe, and by August 21 all Spanish troops and settlers had left the Southwest.

The Zunis carried out their part of the Pueblo Revolt by killing the resident priest of Halona (according to Zuni oral tradition, another priest was allowed to live because he disavowed his Christianity and became a Zuni), burning the church buildings that they had been forced to build, and expelling Spanish settlers who had intruded on their land. As a defensive measure, the Zunis once again abandoned their villages and moved to a settlement on top of Dowa Yallane, where they remained for more than fifteen years.

In 1692, a Spanish commander named Diego de Vargas led a large force of soldiers from Mexico into Pueblo territory and regained control of most of the towns along the Rio Grande. Vargas traveled west to reconquer the Hopis and the Zunis. When he reached Dowa Yallane, he was received with surprising cordiality by the Zunis. Although Zuni leaders had met with representatives from the nearby Hopis and Keres in order to plan a united defense against the Spanish, the size of the Spanish force that reached Dowa Yallane probably compelled the Zuni leadership to offer instead to live in peace with the intruders. In addition, after the Pueblo Revolt the Zunis had had increasing trouble with raiders from other Native American tribes. The introduction of the horse to America had made the formerly peaceful Navajos and Apaches fearsome foes who could raid a farm, steal crops, livestock, and people, and escape with lightning speed. Comanche and Ute raiders had also moved into the area. The powerful Spanish military probably served to entice the Zunis to agree to become allies with them against the raiders.

But the Zunis had not completely capitulated to the Spanish. When, in 1694, another Spanish contingent approached Dowa Yallane seeking tribute and oaths of obedience, the Zunis successfully fought off the soldiers, inflicting many casualties and causing the army to quickly retreat to Santa Fe. This successful resistance led to rumors in Santa Fe that the Zunis and their allies among the Hopis, Keres, and Apaches planned to attack Spanish settlements. Missionaries added to the tension by complaining that the Zunis refused to convert to Christianity. The missionaries finally formally requested that Diego de Vargas, the governor at Santa Fe, send soldiers against the Zunis, but

Vargas believed the rumors to be false and denied the request. The armed uprising never materialized.

The Spanish nonetheless continued to seek obedience from the Zunis. In 1699, a new governor, Pedro Rodriguez Cubero, sent a delegation to Dowa Yallane in order to have the Zunis renew earlier pledges of peace. The meeting seems to have gone fairly well, for shortly after the Spanish delegation left, the Zunis finally moved down from their defensive settlement on Dowa Yallane. The threat of attacks from both raiders and the Spanish still existed, however, and the Zunis concentrated their population in the town of Halona (later called Zuni by English-speaking Americans), on the assumption that it would be easier to defend one large village than several small settlements scattered over a wide area.

As the defensive design of Halona suggests, although the Zunis had agreed not to fight against the Spanish, they were far from being conquered or even reconquered. Despite tremendous pressure from their would-be conquistadores, the Zunis never acquiesced to foreign control of their government, and at the end of the seventeenth century they remained a free and independent people.

5

Aliens on Native Soil

As the eighteenth century began, the Spanish continued their attempts to increase their authority over the Pueblo Indians. Although they were able to govern the people living in villages along the Rio Grande with relative ease, they had difficulty controlling the Zunis. Since the Zunis lived far from Santa Fe, officials found it too costly to continually send troops to force them to comply with Spanish laws. The Zunis' isolation from the Spanish domain was aided by the fact that Navajos and Apaches inhabited the territory between the Zunis and the Rio Grande. These tribes routinely raided soldiers on the march, and Spanish officials quickly became reluctant to risk troops and supplies by sending them through this dangerous territory to the Zunis.

On the rare occasions that the Spanish visited the Zunis, the Zuni leaders would readily promise to live in peace with the Spanish, to follow Spanish law, to attend Catholic services, and to give up their traditional religious practices. As soon as the authorities returned to Santa Fe, however, the Zunis would ignore all requests for tribute and resume their religious practices. As a result, of the three missions built in Zuni villages by the middle of the seventeenth century, only one, a church at Halona, was rebuilt after the reconquest, and it was seldom used.

Not surprisingly, Franciscan missionaries made only a few permanent converts among the Zunis and other Pueblo Indians. Indeed, although missionaries became a regular sight in Halona, they were usually visiting from other Pueblo villages, and more frequently acted as diplomats than religious leaders. In 1776, a priest named Fray Dominguez wrote about the mission's lack of success:

> Even at the end of so many years since the reconquest, . . . their condition now is almost the same as it was in the beginning, for generally speaking they have preserved some very indecent, and perhaps superstitious customs.
>
> Their repugnance and resistance to most Christian acts is evident, for they perform the duties pertaining to the Church under compulsion, and there are usually many omissions.

In addition to the resistance of the Native Americans themselves, friction between Spanish civil and religious authorities helped the Zunis maintain their isolation and independence. Civilian officials often complained about the lack of progress made by Franciscans among the Pueblo Indians and noted the priests' abusive and illegal practices. Juan Antonio de Ornedal y Masa, an envoy of the Spanish viceroy, listed several improprieties:

> The religious almost totally neglect the Indians, even failing to say mass for them. The missionaries, in violation of the law, fail to learn the Native language and to teach the Indians

the Spanish language. The missionaries forcibly take grain and sheep from the Indians who are also compelled to weave for them wool and cotton without pay. They arbitrarily take from the Indians buffalo skins that they obtain for sheltering themselves and the buckskins that they sell. When the Indians complain of this to the civil authorities, the priests threaten them with whippings and other punishments.

For their part, missionaries repeatedly wrote to the viceroy and recounted abuses by civil authorities against the Pueblo Indians. In 1761, Fray Pedro Serrano complained that officials forced men, women, and children to weave blankets, harvest corn, and perform domestic work. Serrano ended his letter by observing that

> These officials never conduct themselves in any way that yields any benefit to the Indians. . . . We religious suffer many injuries, outrages, and afflictions from the officials if we try to defend the unfortunate Indians in any way. . . . The officials laugh, for they alone are favored and protected [knowing that] the best officials are those who oppress the Indians most.

As a result of the bickering, resistance, and general lack of missionary success, the Franciscans had all but stopped their missionary activity among the Zunis when they were officially recalled by the newly formed Mexican government in 1821.

Although the Zunis never abandoned their own religious and cultural practices, the Zunis and the Spanish did cooperate in some areas. The Zunis generally accepted the presence of priests in their towns and, in keeping with their traditional ideal of generous hospitality toward strangers, even warmly welcomed missionaries and other Spanish visitors. However, if the actions of newcomers violated Zuni norms, the offenders were dealt with decisively. For example, in 1700 a group of Spanish soldiers, accompanied by a missionary and three Spanish settlers, were welcomed into Halona to defend the village against raiders. But the troops and settlers treated the Zunis with disdain and curtness, and behaved licentiously toward the Zuni women. On March 3, 1703, the Zunis decided that they had had enough and killed the three settlers, sparing the missionary because he had behaved well and the soldiers only because they were absent from town that day. The Zunis did not believe that the killings would go unpunished and quickly evacuated once again to Dowa Yallane, but the Spanish had decided by this point that the survival of their colonists depended upon the cultivation of goodwill among the Pueblo Indians. Consequently, the Spanish expedition sent to Dowa Yallane two years later was led by the spared missionary, who made an agreement with the Zunis promising them clemency and military protection. The Zunis promptly moved back to Halona and even sent delegates to a 1706 meeting in Santa Fe between the new Spanish governor and representatives of all the Pueblo tribes (except the militantly anti-Spanish Hopis, who eventually engaged in some minor conflicts with the Zunis because of the latter's cooperation with the Spanish).

After the 1705 agreement, the Zunis even engaged in a temporary military alliance with the Spanish. Throughout the eighteenth century, the Navajos and Apaches carried out several attacks against the village of Halona, with casualties resulting on both sides. In retaliation, Zuni warriors sometimes joined Spanish soldiers in expeditions against the Navajos and Apaches. These joint actions did not, however, create a lasting alliance or bond between the Zunis and Spanish but were rather merely a temporary expedience for the beleaguered and vengeful Zunis. Indeed, by the late eighteenth century Spanish authorities had given up hope of dominating the Zunis and other western Pueblo Indians, and in 1799 only seven Spanish people were recorded as living among the Zunis. Spanish rule in all of the American Southwest finally ended in 1821, when the nation of Mexico won its independence from Spain.

Although the Zunis had remained mostly independent

during the period of Spanish domination, contact with these foreigners had affected their lives in several important ways. They adopted numerous articles of European manufacture, such as metal knives, axes, saws, scissors, nails, pots, and kettles. These metal implements and utensils were more durable than traditional wooden, bone, or clay items.

The Spanish also introduced a number of new crops to the Zunis, which had been brought either from Europe or from Mexico, such as wheat, oats, peaches, apples, melons, tomatoes, and chili. In addition, the Spanish introduced the Zunis to sheep and burros, animals that would greatly alter the Zuni economy. Burros were useful as pack animals, while sheep were valuable sources of both meat and wool. Zuni women spun the wool into yarn and wove it into blankets and clothing, which were sold to Spanish and Mexican traders.

An indirect but profound result of the Spanish invasion was a change in Zuni settlement patterns. Before 1540 the Zunis resided in six villages along the Zuni River, but by the end of the seventeenth century all but one of these villages, Halona (later Zuni), had been abandoned. Due to the large increase in the number of residents in this village, a great deal of new housing was constructed. Rooms were added to existing houses, and new homes were built on hills facing the Zuni River, as well as on flat ground at the edge of the village.

Because of the circumstances under which Halona was expanded, the new buildings changed Halona's design so that it was better suited for military defense. The large, multistoried houses of the village all faced inward around central plazas, which were only accessible through a few narrow passages. Rooms on the ground floor usually had no doors or windows, and to enter a house, a person had to climb up a ladder onto the rooftop and then climb down another ladder through an entrance in the roof. If intruders approached the village, the ladders to rooftops could be pulled up, barring access to the rooms and their inhabitants below.

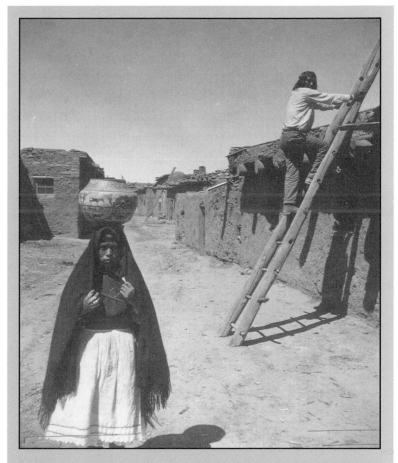

By the end of the 1600s, the Zunis had abandoned their traditional settlement patterns, having mostly consolidated in the town of Halona (which would later become Zuni). In order to safeguard houses from the Spanish, one had to climb up a ladder (shown here) onto the rooftop and then climb down another ladder through an entrance in the roof.

The crops and animals introduced by the Spanish also affected settlement patterns. Once people owned large numbers of sheep, they needed to devote a good deal of time to grazing the animals and had to turn part of their land into pasture for sheep. At the same time, the introduction of the burro meant that fairly large amounts of produce or supplies could be easily carried long distances from a field to the village or vice

versa. As a result of these two developments, in the early eighteenth century the Zunis established several small farming
communities and herding camps a substantial distance from
Halona. At first these communities and camps were inhabited
only during the summer, but three of the communities became
permanent later in the century. The village farthest from
Halona was called Nutria (or *toya* in Zuni) and was located
twenty-five miles northeast of Halona along the Nutria River.
Ojo Caliente (or *kapkwayina,* meaning "water comes up from
the depths") was established fifteen miles to the southwest of
Halona, and Pescado (or *heshota cina,* meaning "marked
house") was situated east of Halona on the Pescado River.

Yet another change that occurred during the period of
Spanish influence was the establishment of civilian government
in Zuni villages. Prior to the Spanish invasion, religious leaders
governed the towns through their appointment of a pekwin.
After the reconquest of 1692, the Spanish set up a council of
civil authorities that operated as a parallel council to the traditional leadership, which retained control over religious and
moral matters. The civilian government included a governor, a
lieutenant governor, and a village council. At first the Spanish
appointed the head of the Bow Priesthood as governor, but by
the middle of the nineteenth century the governor, lieutenant
governor, and councillors were chosen by Zuni religious elders.
Although civilian and religious leaders had separate duties,
they were installed in office through similar ceremonies. The
head of the Rain Priesthood installed the traditional pekwin
and also gave the oath of office to the civilian governor. And
just as the pekwin received a ceremonial staff of feathers as a
symbol of his office, the civilian governor was given a wooden
cane as his symbol of office.

Finally, a tragic result of contact between the Zunis and the
Spanish was the introduction of deadly diseases of European
origin. Before Europeans arrived in North America, the organisms that cause smallpox, measles, and influenza did not exist

on the continent. Since the Zunis and other Native Americans had never been exposed to these diseases, they had not developed any natural resistances or immunities to them. Consequently, when the organisms were brought to America by the Europeans, they spread quickly and with deadly force among the vulnerable indigenous population.

Throughout North America, millions of Native Americans died during widespread epidemics that erupted soon after contact with Europeans. The Zunis were no exception, and several devastating epidemics of smallpox and measles struck Zuni communities in the sixteenth and seventeenth centuries. Although population figures for the early years of the Spanish invasion are not completely reliable, the Zuni population may have been as high as 10,000 in the mid-sixteenth century. By the time of the Pueblo Revolt in 1680, their population had declined to 2,500. The population decreases continued, and by the end of the eighteenth century the Zunis numbered only 1,600. Their population did not begin to increase again until late in the nineteenth century.

When the Spanish left the Southwest in 1821, the Mexican government assumed jurisdiction over the region. The government declared that Native Americans were full citizens of Mexico and that their rights as citizens would be protected. But the Mexican authorities had no effective contact with the Zunis and other Pueblo Indians, who lived in what was then a marginal, outlying province of a new nation. This proved beneficial to the Zunis, who were able to practice their traditions free from official interference or harassment.

Even before the Mexican government gained control in the Southwest, however, intruders from the United States began to enter Zuni territory. A Creole trader named Baptiste Lalande arrived in the Southwest in 1804, followed in 1821 by William Becknell, who set up trading operations in Santa Fe. Shortly afterward, American fur trappers entered the region, purchasing food and supplies from the Native Americans.

Such commerce between Mexican citizens and foreigners was illegal under Mexican laws, but American merchants, attracted to Halona's reputation as a center for intertribal trade, tried to establish trade networks with the Zunis. But because the Americans were primarily interested in valuable beaver furs and the supply of beavers in the Southwest was very small, trade between the Zunis and Americans was not particularly profitable, and by 1835 most of the American traders had left the region.

Mexican jurisdiction over the Southwest was threatened with the outbreak of the Mexican War between the United States and Mexico in the mid-1840s. In addition to fighting with the Mexicans, U.S. troops in the Southwest fought a number of battles with Navajo raiders. In 1846, while in pursuit of some Navajo horse thieves, a group of about sixty U.S. soldiers happened upon Zuni Pueblo. The Zunis were delighted to find a common enemy of the Navajos, and the tribe fed and housed the soldiers in a most congenial manner. A report of the encounter between the Zunis and Americans, written by a private in the army unit involved, noted:

> As soon as our horses were unsaddled, [the Zunis] furnished us with a house, and took us all off to different houses to eat. I went to one house where they set out a soup made with mutton and various kinds of vegetables, and a kind of bread as thin as paper. They have the reputation of being the most hospitable people in the world, which I believe they merit in every respect.
>
> We were out of provision and proposed to buy from them but they said they did not sell their provisions and more particularly to Americans. So they brought in sufficient bread and meal to last our party into camp, which is three days from here. Our saddles, bridles, and all equipment was left exposed to them, but in the morning, not a single article was gone. Where can such a mass of honest people be found?

In 1848, Lai-iu-ah-tsai-ah (shown here in 1879, bottom right), who served as governor of the Zunis from 1830 to 1878, signed a peace treaty with the Navajos and the U.S. government. The treaty called for the Zunis' rights of private property and freedom of religion to be protected by the New Mexico and U.S. governments.

The cordial meeting was climaxed with an exchange of official pledges of peace and friendship between the U.S. Army officers and the Zuni governor Lai-iu-ah-tsai-ah.

The Mexican War ended with Mexico's defeat in 1848. The *Treaty of Guadalupe Hidalgo*, signed by both countries after the war, granted the United States possession of the present-day states of New Mexico and Arizona. The treaty also contained a clause wherein the U.S. government promised to respect the land and rights of the indigenous inhabitants of its new possession. That same year, Lai-iu-ah-tsai-ah and other Zuni leaders met with Navajo leaders and U.S. Army Lieutenant Colonel Henderson P. Boyakin to sign a three-way peace treaty between the Zunis, Navajos, and Americans. The treaty stated in part that the Zunis "shall be protected in the full management of all their rights of Private Property and Religion . . . [by] the authorities, civil and military, of New Mexico and the United States."

By the middle of the nineteenth century, the Zunis had been exposed to three foreign governments, each with its own plans for the indigenous peoples. Despite the turnover in outside powers, the Zunis had managed to maintain their own security and continue their traditional way of living, and when faced with a new would-be overlord, they had obtained treaties and agreements that explicitly protected their rights and properties. But the government, people, and traditions of the United States would put entirely new pressures on Zuni society, pressures that no treaty could contain.

6

Losses and Recoveries

One year after the United States signed a treaty with the Zunis, the tribe was visited by the superintendent of Indian affairs for the area, James Calhoun. Calhoun expressed his desire to maintain friendly relations with the Zunis, and the Zuni leaders expressed their hope of living in peace. The friendly relations between the two governments were further cemented in 1863, when President Abraham Lincoln presented Acoma Pueblo Governor Mariano with a silver-knobbed ebony cane, which thereafter became the ceremonial cane of office.

But relations were far from ideal. The discovery of gold in California in 1848 brought a stream of travelers across Zuni lands. Most of these people were just passing through on their way to California, but some of them stole crops and livestock from Zuni farms. In addition, a number of people stayed in the area, enough so that the U.S. Congress organized the area as the Territory of New Mexico in 1850.

The 1850s also saw several expeditions of scientists and technicians sent by the U.S. government to conduct geographic surveys of New Mexico. A researcher named Baldwin Mollhausen described the Zunis' prosperity at the time. He wrote:

> They breed sheep, keep horses and asses, and practice agriculture on an extensive scale. In all directions, fields of wheat and maize, as well as gourds and melons, bore testimony to their industry. In gardens, they raise beans and onions. And the women are skillful in the art of weaving, and manufacture durable blankets.

These expeditions were not sent out to observe the Zunis, however, but to find feasible land routes to California. A road linking New Mexico with southern California was quickly built that passed near Zuni; since the towns and forts that sprung up near the tribe were the first American settlements of any size east of Los Angeles, the Zunis began to see more and more travelers who stopped in the area to get provisions.

Other expeditions were sent by the U.S. government for the sole purpose of observing the Zunis and other Pueblo Indians. Beginning in the 1870s, the U.S. Bureau of American Ethnology sent teams to contact Native Americans in the region and study their societies. The writings of these *ethnologists* excited a great deal of national attention, and as a result increasing numbers of white American tourists began to visit Zuni territory. But the American ethnologists did not simply write about the Zunis, they also took material artifacts of Zuni culture, such as pots, prayer sticks, and masks, to send or sell to museums. The sheer scale of some of these collecting expeditions—in 1881 one team alone shipped more than 3,700 items of Zuni manufacture and more than 3,000 items of Hopi manufacture to the Smithsonian National Museum in Washington, D.C.—rendered them comparable to the early Spanish tribute-collecting expeditions. Some of these items were purchased

Beginning in the 1870s, American ethnologists (those who study cultural anthropology) began taking Zuni artifacts, such as this Zuni fetish bowl, from Zuni territory. In 1881, alone, more than 3,700 Zuni artifacts were shipped to the Smithsonian Institution in Washington, D.C.; many of which were from sacred sites.

from willing sellers, but many were sacred items that were simply seized or stolen from the tribe.

During the 1870s, increasing numbers of American missionaries arrived in the area with the purpose of converting the Zunis to various sects of Christianity. A group of Mormon missionaries founded a permanent settlement on the boundary of Zuni territory in 1876, and in response the Presbyterians built a mission and school just north of Zuni the following year. Neither sect met with much success: During this time, Mormons were viewed with suspicion and hostility by U.S. authorities, who actively discouraged the Zunis from becoming Mormons, and few Zuni parents wanted the foreigners at the Presbyterian school to supervise their children's education (although attendance increased somewhat after the Presbyterians began passing out free lunches to the pupils). The missionaries were all quite vocal in condemning traditional Zuni religious beliefs and practices, and they frequently demanded that the U.S. government outlaw traditional Zuni rituals, much to the consternation of the tribe. Zuni religious practices were ultimately not made illegal, but the Zunis began to conduct formerly public ceremonies in private to avoid such censure.

Naturally, American traders accompanied the large flow of people. During the 1870s, three white American and two Native American traders established operations at Zuni. At first trade was fairly limited, and traders exchanged manufactured goods for traditional items, such as agricultural produce, cloth, jewelry, and pottery. But commerce expanded after 1881 when the Atlantic and Pacific Railroad completed a track to the town of Gallup, New Mexico, located forty miles northeast of Zuni. Once the railroad was opened, the traders began to purchase sheep and cattle to ship by railroad to national markets in eastern and western states. As a result, the Zunis began to raise more herds, which they sold for cash that they used to buy American products.

While the Zunis were increasing their livestock holdings, American sheepherders and cattle ranchers entered the Southwest looking for grazing pasture. A steady influx of settlers who encroached on Zuni territory led to increased hostility and competition between the Zunis and the outsiders. As more outsiders arrived, the Zunis demanded that the U.S. government fulfill its obligations under the Treaty of Guadalupe Hidalgo to protect their land. Problems arose immediately because the exact extent of Zuni territory had never been properly surveyed and registered with the U.S. government, and in 1877, when President Rutherford B. Hayes issued an executive order that created the Zuni Reservation, the area of land encompassed within the *reservation* was only about one-tenth the size of territory the Zunis had traditionally occupied. Many landmarks and areas considered sacred to the Zunis were not included in the reservation boundaries, and many Zunis felt no particular obligation to quit using land they had always regarded as their own because of a proclamation made in some far-off city to the east.

Because of a surveying error, the reservation's borders also did not include several of the Zunis' small farming settlements, among them the village of Nutria and its nearby springs, which were vital to Zuni agriculture. A group of U.S. Army officers stationed at nearby Fort Wingate had earlier set up a ranch just east of the borders of Zuni territory called the Cibola Cattle Company. When they discovered the surveying error, the officers (who were infamous among the Zunis for illegally grazing their cattle on reservation lands) attempted to gain title to Nutria and its springs. One of the officers was the son-in-law of a powerful Illinois senator and presidential hopeful named John Logan, who on a tour of the American Southwest had informed the officers of the opportunity to obtain the valuable land. The eastern newspapers were tipped off to the affair by a researcher sent by the Bureau of American Ethnology and an adopted Zuni named Frank Cushing; the result was a tremendous scandal that pitted Logan's vociferous political supporters against his equally vocal opponents. An early casualty of this battle was Cushing, who was finally forced to leave the region by Logan in 1884. (Cushing would later return and continued his entire life to speak out on behalf of the Zunis.)

Fortunately for the Zunis, Senator Logan's land-grab occurred when the tribe actually exercised considerable influence in the East. The Zunis had been the subject of many a flattering popular book and magazine article, beginning with the memoirs of the soldiers who had been hosted by the Zunis during the Mexican War, and had captured the interest and sympathy of many white Americans. In addition, Cushing had arranged a well-publicized tour of the eastern states for several Zuni leaders in 1882. The party had traveled to Chicago, Boston, and Washington D.C., meeting President Chester Arthur and a number of other highly prominent intellectual and business leaders. Many of these influential easterners were favorably impressed by the tribal leaders and became advocates of Zuni land protection; as a result of their efforts, a second

A Visit to the East

In 1882 and again in 1886, five Zuni leaders took a trip to eastern cities in the United States. They wanted to visit places that they had heard of and to see where the white people who were surrounding their lands in New Mexico had originally come from. They had also heard stories of the eastern ocean (the Atlantic) and wanted to see for themselves its great expanse and to take back some of the water from what they called the "Ocean of the Sunrise." This name had great symbolic significance for them because of the sacredness of water to a people inhabiting arid lands and because of the spiritual meaning of the eastern direction, the direction of the sun and its powerful life-giving energy.

On their first trip, the Zunis toured Washington, D.C., where they met President Chester A. Arthur and then went by train to Boston, passing through Baltimore and Philadelphia. On their second visit in 1886, the Zunis were invited to spend several months in Massachusetts near the Atlantic coast. Both trips were arranged and accompanied by anthropologist Frank Cushing, who lived many years among the Zunis in the Southwest. In addition to helping his Zuni hosts, Cushing wanted to raise funds to carry out extensive archaeological and anthropological expeditions to the Southwest.

The Zuni visitors were impressed by the sights and sounds of the large American cities and witnessed firsthand the dominant power and wealth of the United States. They reflected on the personalities and the values of American culture. In particular, they voiced amazement at Americans' desire for other people's lands and their individual competitiveness. These traits of executive order was issued in 1883 that added the outlying farm areas, including Nutria and its springs, to the reservation area. A later trip made in 1886 by the Zuni governor and two of his aides helped further publicize the Zunis' cause.

But tours of eastern cities did not prevent both Anglo and Hispanic settlers and ranchers from making more and more inroads into traditional Zuni territories that did not legally

greed and envy violated basic Zuni personality ethics that stressed cooperation and hospitality. In the words of Heluta, one of the Zuni travelers:

Such indeed are the Americans. Though we Indians live in a poor and dried up country, though we may love them not, yet they gather around us and coming to our country continually, and even strive to get our land from us. Is it possible for anyone to say what they want? Where is there a country more beautiful than this we are sitting in now? Is there any water needed here? Without irrigation, things grow green, and there is water to drink . . . But the sentiment of home affects them not; the little bits of land they may own, or the house they may have been bred in, are as nothing to them: for they wander incessantly, wander through all difficulties and dangers, to seek new places and better things. Why is it they are so unceasingly unsatisfied?*

Another Zuni visitor, Palowahtiwa, responded, "Above every people they are a people of emulation, a people of fierce jealousies . . . And if one American goes one day's journey in the direction of a difficult trail, it is not long ere another American will go two day's journey in the direction of a more difficult one. One American cannot bear that another shall surpass him."**

* Frank Cushing, *Zuni: Selected Writings of Frank Hamilton Cushing*, ed. Jesse Green (Lincoln, Nebr.: University of Nebraska Press, 1979), 414–416.

** Ibid., 416.

form part of the Zuni Reservation. Toward the end of the nineteenth century this encroachment became especially severe on the eastern and southern portions of Zuni land; in the western portion the Mormons were also expanding their holdings. As the population of immigrant communities grew, the Zuni lost access to most of their former territory, especially areas located near springs and streams, which were especially desirable to settlers. These new settlements prevented the Zunis from grazing their animals, hunting, and gathering wild plants in familiar places that they had used for centuries. Not surprisingly, the result was a number of conflicts over land use, some of them bloody.

American companies also began exploiting the natural resources in Zuni territory during the late 1800s. Timber companies started clear-cutting large portions of forest in the Zuni Mountains in the 1890s. In just over ten years, more than two billion feet of timber were cut—and once the trees were gone, white American cattle and sheep owners grazed their animals on the deforested land, eliminating any chance of reforestation.

Other Native American groups were also competing for Zuni land. Navajos and Apaches seeking refuge from U.S. Army troops and aggressive white American settlers entered Zuni territory in the mid- and late nineteenth century and resumed raiding Zuni farms and villages. In one especially serious incident in 1850, more than one hundred Navajos held the village of Zuni under siege for sixteen days. The Zunis later retaliated by killing thirty Navajos, and Zuni guides and spies assisted U.S. troops in their war against the Navajos (although Zuni traders were an important source of supplies for both Navajo and Apache tribes during their wars with the United States).

The conflicts between the Zunis, Navajos, and Apaches reflected the crowding all Native American groups were experiencing as American settlers, backed by U.S. troops, moved onto their lands. Both Navajos and Apaches had been forced out of their traditional territories, and it mattered little to

U.S. authorities if the land available for them to live on had historically belonged to another tribe. Eventually the Navajos settled in the northern areas of traditional Zuni territory, while the Apaches settled in the southern and western sections. In 1868, the U.S. government established boundaries for a Navajo reservation that included a northern section of traditional Zuni territory, and three years later, some Apaches settled on a reservation that took in a southwestern area of traditional Zuni lands. The establishment of such new reservations forced the Zunis to confine themselves more to their relatively small reservation area during a time when their population was finally beginning to increase after centuries of decline.

The Zunis were also faced with increased efforts by missionaries and U.S. government officials to interfere with their traditional religious life. In 1897, Mary E. DeSette, the teacher at the Presbyterian day school, had several Bow Priests arrested for persecuting a witch. (She was entirely unaware of and probably equally unconcerned about the complex nature of the crime of witchcraft in Zuni society.) DeSette, who had previously distinguished herself by instigating a haircutting campaign (Zuni men wore long hair) and by threatening to cancel the Shalako festival, was a deeply disruptive force on the reservation, mainly because she felt that the Zunis would respect her and accept her authority only if she, as she put it in a letter to the U.S. Commissioner of Indian Affairs, "stir[red] up the authorities" at every possible occasion. In keeping with this philosophy, DeSette arranged for U.S. Army troops to aid the local sheriff in arresting the Bow Priests, and although the charges against the priests were dropped and they were released by the government after only a few months (and after having had their hair cut off), at DeSette's request the troops occupied Zuni for nearly a year. According to historian C. Gregory Crampton in *The Zunis of Cibola*, "throughout the affair the Zunis remained calm, though they may well have had some misgivings about future trends in education." The presence of

U.S. troops acting as law enforcement seriously undermined the authority of the Bow Priests; this erosion of authority was intensified because those priests who had had their hair cut off in prison were considered defiled and could no longer participate in important religious ceremonies.

Not surprisingly, the Presbyterian mission did not attract huge numbers of converts at this time, nor did the Christian (Dutch) Reformed Church, which established a mission at Zuni in 1897. As in past centuries, the Zunis' participation in traditional religious societies and rituals oriented their lives around common activities and shared meanings, and giving up such meaningful religious traditions did not come easily. In addition, the common demand that Christian converts give up any involvement in traditional Zuni religious practices was completely antithetical to many Zunis, who held that the different religious beliefs were not entirely incompatible. As one missionary lamented, "the most common reaction of Zunis to the gospel message is that the Jesus-way and the Zuni-way are 'hi-ni-na,' 'the same.'"

During the late nineteenth and early twentieth centuries, the U.S. government became more directly involved in regulating the education of Native Americans in general. The federal government had decided that attempts should be made to "civilize" Native Americans by having Native American children attend schools where they could learn American customs and values. English-language instruction was viewed as critical to this effort; consequently, the use of Native languages was banned in schools. The U.S. commissioner of Indian affairs clearly enunciated reasons for this policy as far back as 1887, stating:

> Instruction of Indians in the vernacular is not only of no use to them but is detrimental to the cause of education and civilization and will not be permitted in any Indian school. This language which is good enough for a white person ought to be good enough for the red person. It is also believed that

teaching Indians in their own barbarous dialect is a positive detriment to them. The impracticability, if not impossibility of civilizing Indians in any other tongue than our own would seem obvious.

After the DeSette affair of 1897, the U.S. government took closer control of the schools at Zuni, ending the subsidizing of mission schools and opening a government day school instead. In addition to the day school, the U.S. government opened a boarding school in 1907, and the Christian (Dutch) Reformed Church opened a nonsubsidized mission day school in 1908. These schools offered basic subjects, such as writing and reading, cooking and sewing for girls, and manual skills for boys. Such formal education became relatively popular early on, in part because there were now a number of schools on the reservation, so a student who had trouble adjusting at one school could always transfer to a different one. The English-only policy of these schools was initially supported by the Zunis, who felt that their children would learn Zuni at home anyway and that knowledge of English would be a valuable skill when negotiating among Americans. In later years, however, the Zunis would pressure their schools into becoming more bilingual and placing more emphasis on Zuni culture.

The twentieth century saw yet another expansion of Zuni agriculture, as Zuni farmers adopted American technology, such as plows and iron hoes, shovels, and rakes. Agricultural surpluses were sold for a profit to American traders and residents of nearby towns, such as Gallup, New Mexico, and Holbrook, Arizona. The Zunis also sold corn, wheat, and other farm products to soldiers at Fort Defiance and Fort Wingate. Dams and reservoirs were constructed on the Zuni River during the 1900s, creating a more regular supply of water for irrigation. The boom in Zuni farming led to the establishment of a new farming settlement in 1912 called Tekapo (meaning "full of hills"), located southwest of Zuni on the Zuni River.

Shown here is Zuni Pueblo, circa 1911. By the early part of the twentieth century, the village had changed a great deal from the time of the Spanish. Many one-story houses were constructed, along with ground-level doors and windows, because the Zunis no longer had to worry about protecting themselves from outside invaders.

Zuni ranching also prospered in the early twentieth century. By 1910, Zuni ranchers owned approximately 65,000 head of sheep, more than double the number they had in 1880. The Zuni Reservation contained about 285,000 acres, and as the herds grew, the problem of finding adequate land to graze them on became critical. Zuni leaders and *agents* of the federal *Bureau of Indian Affairs* (BIA) repeatedly asked the president and Congress to enlarge the reservation, but instead of adding to Zuni territory, Congress took land away from the reservation in 1910 to create national forests in the area. The Zunis protested, and two years later President William Taft reversed the decision, returning the land. Finally, in 1917, President Woodrow Wilson issued an executive order that added about 80,000 acres to the Zuni Reservation. Additional acreage was included in 1935, bringing the total area up to approximately 340,000 acres, and in 1940, bringing the total above 400,000 acres. In addition to traditional agricultural sources of income, some Zunis worked for railroads, government agencies, and businesses located in nearby Anglo towns.

Changes also took place in the village of Zuni itself. Although the basic design of Zuni houses did not change, new houses were built with larger rooms and higher ceilings. Defensive concerns were no longer paramount, so ground-level doors and windows became common. In addition, many of the upper-story dwellings were taken down, and more ground-level homes were built. The Zunis no longer had to cluster all their buildings together for defensive purposes, so outlying houses, built at some distance from the main village, became more common, with 81 families (about 37 percent of the population) living in these "suburbs" by 1915.

The local system of Zuni government also reflected both continuity and change as the twentieth century progressed. At the beginning of the century, the two governing councils—one consisting of religious leaders whose decisions were enforced by the Bow Priests and one entirely secular in nature, consisting of a governor, a lieutenant governor, and councillors—coexisted and shared power. But the authority of the Bow Priests, already threatened by the DeSette affair, was further undermined when the U.S. government decided to exercise closer control over the Zunis by opening a local BIA office near Zuni in 1902. The new Zuni agency was headed by an agent who supervised federal programs and local activities. BIA agents also advised Zuni secular leaders and had authority to approve or veto decisions of the council.

In 1916, the BIA agent to the Zunis became involved in a controversy that deeply affected Zuni politics. That year a group of Catholic clergy proposed to build a new mission in Zuni. When a public meeting was called to discuss the request, all in attendance signaled their opposition by a voice vote.

However, a small group of Zuni Roman Catholics appealed to the BIA agent (himself a Roman Catholic), who donated a plot of village land for the construction of the church. The church, named St. Anthony's Mission Church, was completed in 1922, over the opposition of the majority of the Zunis. Zunis opposed to the mission became known as Protestants (although many were not practitioners of any Christian religion), while those who supported the mission became known as Catholics (whether or not they were actually Roman Catholic)—a political division that has continued to the present day.

In 1928, a U.S. government study known as the *Meriam Report* revealed that many Native American tribes lived in abysmally poor conditions. These conditions would be improved, the report suggested, by increased federal funding to the tribes, as well as greater tribal control over how such funds were spent. As a result of these findings, Commissioner of Indian Affairs John Collier urged Congress to pass new legislation to give tribal governing councils authority over development programs on their reservations. Although Collier was willing to hand over a considerable amount of power to the tribal councils, he also wanted to regulate their functioning and establish guidelines for selection of councillors in a manner that was not always consistent with tribal traditions.

With Collier's urging, Congress passed legislation known as the *Indian Reorganization Act* (IRA) in 1934. The IRA provided that the reservations adopt formal constitutions and elect their tribal leaders. Each reservation had the option of accepting or rejecting the IRA's provisions through a local referendum. Andrew Trotter, the BIA superintendent in charge of the Zuni Agency, was instrumental in convincing the Zunis— who at the time were in the midst of a bitter dispute between the Catholics and the Protestants that threatened to render the village ungovernable—to adopt the IRA provisions. Once the IRA was accepted, Trotter appointed a nominating committee of six members to nominate two candidates for the position of governor. After the nominations were made, a public meeting was held at which all men in attendance could vote. The candidate who received the most votes became governor, while the losing candidate became lieutenant governor. In addition to the gubernatorial election, six members of a tribal council were also selected, each representing a different district. Under the new regulations, all tribal leaders served for terms of one year. The nominating committee appointed by Trotter functioned for two years, after which members of the committee were elected by male voters until 1965, when women obtained the franchise. Obviously, this new system of choosing leaders was extremely different from the traditional system, wherein religious leaders appointed the members of the local government. According to C. Gregory Crampton, "The transition from a theocratic form of government to one based on popular consent was not achieved without much division and debate, anxiety, stress, tension, and soul-searching. People still take sides on the form of government the Zunis should have."

The 1930s witnessed other federal initiatives that also had long-term consequences for the Zunis. For the first time since the reservation was established in 1877, the U.S. government carried out an extensive survey of the boundaries of Zuni land. When the survey was completed in 1934, government workers erected a fence around the reservation's borders. Prior to this time, Zuni herders had routinely grazed their animals in adjacent pastures, but after the reservation was fenced in, they were restricted to the land within the reservation. This reduction in grazing area quickly resulted in a depletion of good forage and erosion of the soil. In response to the worsening situation, Collier instituted a program of stock reduction aimed at limiting the number of animals owned by Native Americans. The Zuni Reservation was divided into eighteen grazing units, and each was given a quota of livestock based on what federal authorities thought the unit could sustain. If herders in the unit had holdings that exceeded the limit, they were forced to sell the surplus animals to the U.S. government at fixed prices.

The Zunis vigorously protested the stock-reduction program. Zuni herders had never been consulted during the development of this program, and they resented what they saw as a high-handed interference with their livelihood. Many families had to give up a large portion of their herds, thereby losing a stable source of income. The prices paid herders for their sheep by the U.S. government were low, and a one-time payment for herds did not reflect the sheep's true value, because herders sold wool from the same animals year after year. Despite these losses, Zuni herders made a slow economic recovery after World War II.

The 1940s also saw more than two hundred Zuni men leave the village to fight for the United States in World War II. Many of them were exposed to new countries and new cultures, and some of them came back expounding ideas and exhibiting behavior their elders found distinctly non-Zuni, which resulted for a short while in a good deal of generational friction. The veterans quickly reintegrated themselves into Zuni life, however, participating in dances and religious ceremonies and utilizing their G.I. benefits to obtain vocational and agricultural training. By the mid-twentieth century, the Zunis had adjusted to changed conditions brought about by pressures from outside forces, incorporating new technologies and activities into their lives while keeping faith in their own values and beliefs.

7

Contemporary Issues

The Zuni Reservation currently consists of 418,304 acres, or more than 700 square miles of land and, according to the 2000 U.S. Census, was home to 6,367 people (3,304 women and 3,063 men)—a dramatic recovery in this century from the low of 1,514 people recorded in 1905. Census data also indicates the continued strength of Zuni families: In 1990, 97 percent of the Zunis resided in family-based households, while only 3 percent lived alone or with non-family members. Though these percentages fell in the 2000 Census, the percentage of Zuni households based on family membership was the highest among all U.S. population groups.

Many changes have taken place in the Zunis' lives. The reservation itself has undergone modernization in terms of housing, public services, and transportation. In the 1950s, improvements were made in public services that included the installation of electricity, the construction of a piped water system, the paving of roads, and

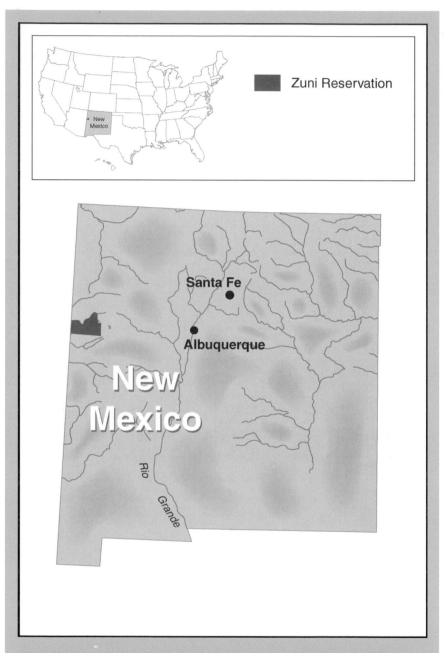

Shown here is a map of the Zuni Reservation, which lies just south of Gallup, New Mexico, along the Arizona border. Today, the Zuni Reservation is home to more than 6,000 Zunis, who live primarily in Zuni Pueblo.

the completion of a sewer system and indoor plumbing. The community of Zuni now contains two distinct types of housing.

In the old central section of town, the houses primarily retain the traditional Zuni designs, although they have been modernized and enlarged. New homes—mostly single-family dwellings, some with small lawns—have been constructed in suburban areas outside Zuni. These homes are of various styles, some with gabled or pitched roofs and some built from wood, cinder block, and other materials. The community at Blackrock, the site of the BIA agency, located several miles to the northeast of Zuni, has also increased in size. An airstrip was built there in 1967, and the community is also now the home of a hospital run by the public health service. The location of traditional kivas and open plazas has remained the same, but new public facilities have been added to Zuni, including a large building that contains the headquarters of the tribal council and other government offices. Five schools now serve the reservation.

The Zuni economy has grown and diversified since the middle of the twentieth century. Sources of income include farming, herding, wage work, and craft production. Farming continues to be an important endeavor, although most rely on farming only for supplemental income. Only about one thousand acres of Zuni land are currently under cultivation, a sharp decrease from the ten thousand to twelve thousand acres farmed a century ago. Major crops today include corn, pinto beans, wheat, chili, cabbage, onions, and beets, which are either consumed in the household or sold to nearby markets. As in past centuries, most farming is done by men, although a number of older women still plant small traditional waffle gardens near their homes.

The Zunis have expanded and upgraded water supplies to increase farm production and livestock holdings, digging numerous wells throughout the reservation to provide water for livestock and developing the natural springs at Nutria, Pescado, and Ojo Caliente. Approximately 95 percent of the reservation's land is now used for grazing. The reservation is divided into 95 grazing units for sheepherding, each assigned to a specific herder or group of herders. Four pastures for cattle are assigned to two cattle associations. As of 1992, the Zunis owned some 10,735 sheep, 122 goats, 1,767 cattle, and 32 horses.

All use of grazing land is regulated by provisions of the Zuni Range Code, adopted in 1976. The code issues permits to herders and sets limits for the number of animals allowed in each grazing unit or cattle range. If owners exceed their annual quotas, they must sell the surplus. The Zuni A:shiwi Livestock Committee was formed in 1992 to supervise use of rangelands. It updates and enforces the range code, recommends range improvements, and resolves any conflicts that arise over use of land. Improvements have been made in rangelands through tribal programs that reseed the land, remove unwanted trees, and restore pasture.

The Zunis are developing additional uses of their land in order to provide tribal and individual income. Deposits of sand, gravel, and limestone are mined by public and private concerns for the construction and paving of roads on and near the reservation. At one time the BIA operated four mines to exploit the substantial coal deposits near Nutria and Pescado. These mines are now defunct but may be reopened in the future, as may the historic copper mines in the Zuni Mountains. The Zunis have also stocked their reservoirs with fish for recreational purposes.

Most Zuni families support themselves through wage work. Even among families who are engaged in farming or herding, some members usually have jobs and contribute their salaries to the household. Some people work in the public sector, in office or maintenance positions for tribal and federal agencies. Others seek employment in local businesses and industries or tribal enterprises. And some work in nearby towns (especially Gallup) as construction workers, nurses, and employees of restaurants and stores. Despite the range of jobs, rates of unemployment and underemployment are high among the Zunis because the actual number of jobs in the area is fairly low.

Many Zunis are self-employed as silversmiths or artisans. Silver work, which began as an occupation for men, is now practiced by women as well, and in many cases, husbands and wives form a team, allocating separate tasks in the process of jewelry-making to each spouse. Zuni silversmiths produce jewelry in two distinctive styles, needlepoint and inlay. In the needlepoint style, small bits of turquoise are cut and mounted in silver to form patterns on rings, necklaces, bracelets, and pins. In the inlay technique, small pieces of shell, coral, jet, and turquoise are cut into different shapes and then mounted in a base of silver. Silversmiths sell their jewelry to traders in Gallup, Santa Fe, Albuquerque, and many other cities. Two organizations, the Zuni Craftsmen's Cooperative Association and the Zuni Arts and Crafts Enterprise, market jewelry to both local and national outlets and promote silversmiths, potters, painters, and sculptors.

Some Zuni artists produce objects called *fetishes* that have great religious significance. Fetishes are representative images of deities made of wood and decorated with paint and feathers. Zuni artists have been making sacred fetishes for centuries, but many of the older fetishes were bought or stolen from the tribe by visitors and were eventually acquired by museums and private galleries and collectors. In 1978, the Zunis began to seek the return of their sacred objects, and by 1992, sixty-three such objects had been returned by museums such as the Smithsonian Institution in Washington, D.C., the Museum of the American Indian in New York City, and the Museum of New Mexico in Albuquerque. Private galleries and individual collectors have also returned several fetishes. Another result of the Zunis' efforts to repossess their fetishes was the passage in

Many Zunis are self-employed and work as silversmiths. Shown here is Della Casi, a jewelry-maker from Zuni Pueblo.

Congress of the *Native American Graves Protection and Repatriation Act of 1990*, which provides for the return of Native American artifacts and grave remains to the tribe from which they were taken.

The political structure of the tribe underwent a good deal of change during the 1970s. In 1970, the Zunis adopted a formal constitution, and the U.S. government recognized the *Zuni Tribal Council* as the Zunis' official legislative and executive body, with the right to control the local government and organize elections. In 1974, the Zunis eliminated the nominating committee and instituted popular elections in which candidates run on their own behalf. The governor, lieutenant governor, and members of the tribal council are now elected to four-year terms. The current governor, Arlen Quetawki, Sr., was first elected to office in 2002 and is serving his first term.

One area of critical concern for the tribal council, and for all Zunis, is land rights and compensation for land taken illegally during the past centuries. The Zunis lobbied for the return of Zuni Salt Lake, which not only provides salt but is an important religious site. In 1978, the U.S. Congress enacted legislation directing the federal government to acquire Zuni Salt Lake from the State of New Mexico and to return it to the tribe. The late Robert Lewis, who served as governor of Zuni Pueblo on and off for nearly three decades, was among those legislatures who helped return Zuni Salt Lake to its rightful owners.

A dispute over another sacred area ended in victory for the Zunis in the 1980s. The tribe filed a suit for the return of a site called Koluwala-wa, located at the juncture of the Zuni and Little Colorado rivers. Koluwala-wa is the focus of pilgrimages made every four years by religious leaders who ask deities there for rain to nurture the land and crops, and it is one of the places where Zuni souls go after death. In 1984, the Zunis won the return of Koluwala-wa, but they were sometimes denied access to the area by ranchers who owned surrounding land. After years of protest in court, the Zunis were granted the permanent right to cross private land on their ritual journeys to Koluwala-wa.

In addition to suits for the return of land, the Zunis submitted a claim to the U.S. Court of Claims in 1978 for monetary compensation for land taken from them in the nineteenth and twentieth centuries. The Court of Claims issued a ruling in 1987 giving the Zunis title to a large portion of present-day Arizona and New Mexico and stating that the tribe had been wrongfully deprived of 14,835,892 acres of their land during

(continued on page 92)

Zuni Conservation Project

The Zuni Conservation Project was established in 1992 as mandated by the Zuni Land Conservation Act of 1990, which settled a land claims dispute against the United States brought by the Zuni tribe. The project is charged with developing programs to restore land damaged by decades and centuries of misuse and encroachment by outsiders, as well as to plan and implement projects aimed at sustainable resource development. A list of the projects underway or in planning stages gives an overview of the kinds of issues that Zunis consider important for the maintenance and development of their territory and their culture.

Watershed Restoration

These projects are aimed at repairing land and restoring the Zuni watershed. Particularly in the arid Southwest, watershed restoration depends on land management policies. For the Zunis, land management focuses on farming and grazing livestock, especially sheep and cattle. Some of the projects include:

Watershed treatments;
Tribal Forest treatments;
Repairs to erosion control structures;
Peach orchard rehabilitation;
Protection and development of natural springs;
Fish and wildlife wetland and meadow development.

Hydrology

The water resources of Zuni territory are relatively limited, especially lacking year-round flowing rivers, although there are a number of small springs. Additional water for irrigating crops and replenishing the soil comes from rain and groundwater. The Zuni tribe recognizes that its growing population will put additional strain on resources. Therefore, water sources need to be protected in quality and developed in quantity. Hydrology projects include:

Coordination of flood early warning system;
Rangeland water development designs;
Assistance to Zuni Solid Waste Program;
Technical support to Zuni Water Rights Program;
Assistance in sewage treatment and artificial wetland planning.

Geographic Information Systems

The Zuni Tribe is developing a computerized system to help manage resources, collect data, and coordinate programs concerning irrigation, agricultural fields, and grazing lands. They are mapping the growth of crops, grazing units, and water resources.

Range Conservation

The Zuni tribe is concerned with managing rangeland, recognizing that most available grazing lands are located in arid or semi-arid areas with sparse grass and shrubs, factors conducive to high levels of erosion. Conservation projects include:

Range water development;
Annual vegetation surveys;
Windmill repair;
Review of range carrying capacity data and policy.

Sustainable Agriculture

Today, only a small number of Zunis are continuing their tradition of farming. Most Zuni farmers grow vegetables, alfalfa, and other forage crops in small gardens near their houses. However, the Zuni tribe is responding to renewed interest in farming by developing projects aimed at sustainable agriculture. Such projects include:

Assistance to Zuni Organic Farmers Cooperative;
Discovery and rehabilitation of old peach orchards;
Developing gardens at community schools;
Maintaining Zuni Community Seedbank;
Maintaining Community Compost Project;
Completion of annual crop surveys.

Community Forests

The Zuni tribe is interested in developing forest resources principally for local use. Projects emphasize the importance of maintaining and expanding forest ecology, especially stands of piñon and juniper, the only types of trees that grow in abundance in Zuni territory.

(*continued from page 89*)
the period from 1876 to 1939. Following years of negotiation, the Zunis were awarded $25 million as compensation for their land. The award was deposited in a trust fund and is awaiting the tribe's decision on how to put it to best use.

In 1990, the Zunis reached an agreement with the U.S. government that ended another legal suit. In the 1970s, the Zunis had sued the U.S. government for neglecting its responsibilities to protect Zuni land, as pledged in the treaties signed between the two nations. The tribe claimed that the U.S. government had illegally sold Zuni land to a number of non-Zunis, including railroad companies that were extending track through the Southwest at the turn of the twentieth century and U.S. officers stationed at Fort Wingate who wished to open private ranches. In addition, the U.S. government permitted ranchers to encroach on and to overgraze Zuni land, and it allowed timber companies to overcut Zuni forests. Finally, the U.S. government permitted the mining of coal and salt from Zuni territory without compensating the tribe.

The Zunis' suit against the United States ended in an agreement ratified by Congress as the *Zuni Land Conservation Act of 1990*, which established a permanent Zuni Indian Resource Development Trust Fund, consisting of $17 million. Interest from the fund is used to create and implement the Zuni Sustainable Resource Development Plan (see sidebar on pages 90–91), aimed at developing renewable resources on the reservation, rehabilitating the reservation's watershed and water resources, and acquiring land for future use. The Zuni Sustainable Resource Development Plan is overseen and implemented by the Zuni Conservation Project, directed by James Enote, which aims to replant vegetation, control soil erosion, improve soil quality, and reduce the loss of water. The Conservation Project collects data on fish and wildlife resources, water sources, and forestry needs, and it began a pilot program at Nutria in 1992 to gather data on local conditions, including the quality of soil, water resources, crop needs, and labor skills of Zuni farmers.

Another land conservation program is the Zuni Sustainable Agriculture Project, dedicated to developing local agriculture. Project workers study soil management issues such as irrigation procedures and soil quality. They are currently investigating the possibility of reestablishing peach orchards originally planted during the period of Spanish conquest on the mesa at Dowa Yallane and expanding production of alfalfa.

Other tribal projects seek to preserve the Zunis' cultural heritage and advance the tribe's opportunities for the future. The A:shiwi A:wan Museum and Heritage Center (*A:shiwi A:wan* means "belonging to the Zuni people") was founded as a center for maintaining, displaying, and enhancing knowledge of Zuni history and culture. In the words of the museum's statement of purpose, it is not a "temple" for the past, but "a community learning center which links the past with the present as a strategy to deal with the future." The museum has a tribal archive that keeps documents of all tribal activities, and it publishes a quarterly newsletter containing information about programs at the museum and elsewhere in the community. News about local events and current issues is also relayed on the Zunis' own radio station, KSHI-FM, founded in 1977.

The Zunis proudly maintain many aspects of their traditional culture. Families are bound together with strong feelings of communal loyalty and support, and matrilineal clans continue to determine an individual's social and group identity. The Zuni language is still the first language of most people. The entire community unites to celebrate sacred rituals that have as much meaning for modern Zunis as they did for their ancestors. In the words of a Zuni storyteller:

> Today as we live in the present ways of our people, we live also within the realm of our ancestors, for we are sustained through the rituals and beliefs of long ago. We live in accordance to the ways of our people, which bring life, blessings, and happiness.

8

The Zunis in the Twenty-First Century

A s the Zunis enter the twenty-first century, they can feel secure in a number of significant successes in their struggle to maintain their lands and their rights of access to sacred places. But although their economy is improving, Zunis still suffer from some of the same economic hardships as most other Native Americans, especially those living in reservation communities.

In August 2003, the Zunis won a major victory in their fight to protect the Zuni Salt Lake, a sacred lake believed to be the home of Salt Woman (also called Salt Mother), one of the people's most revered deities. The lake, located fifty miles southeast of the Zuni Reservation, has for centuries been the destination of pilgrimages by the Zunis as well as by members of other Southwestern indigenous nations. Pilgrims have gone there to seek spiritual advice and make offerings to the deities to show them honor and respect. Zuni Rain Priests have gone to the lake on annual pilgrimages to pray for the

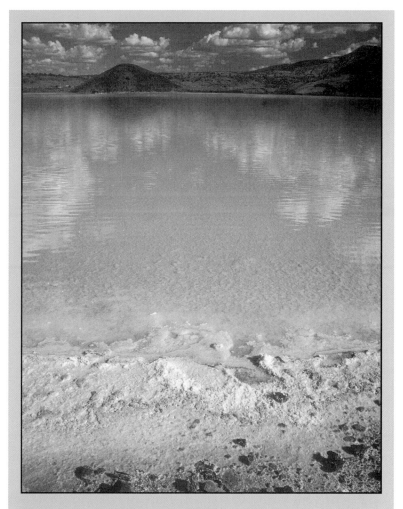

Zuni Salt Lake, located fifty miles southeast of the Zuni Reservation, is sacred to the Zunis. The tribe won back control of the lake from the State of New Mexico in 1986 and won a major victory in 2003 by stopping the Salt River Project, a private utility power company in Arizona, from developing a strip mine near the lake.

rain so necessary in the arid Southwest for the sustenance of their crops and their people. People have also gone there to collect salt from the rich saline water for use in ceremonies as well as for everyday domestic purposes. According to Zuni tradition, the land surrounding the lake has been an area of sanctuary and peace.

The Zuni tribe was awarded control over the land by the U.S. Congress in 1986 but a private utility power company based in Arizona, called Salt River Project (SRP) began to buy land around the Salt Lake in the late 1980s. Their plan was to develop an eighteen-thousand-acre strip mine for coal, only ten miles from the lake. The company's plans included the use of up to eighty-five gallons of water every minute for a period of forty years in order to process the coal. Finally, the plan included a railroad line forty-four miles in length that would extend from their mine to a generating station. The rail line would cut across burial grounds and sacred pilgrimage routes. Even in preliminary stages, the company destroyed Zuni property. During initial survey work, SRP crews unearthed seven bodies of Zuni ancestors who need to be reburied according to Zuni custom.

The Zunis immediately began to protest the plans, citing the sacred value of the lake and its surrounding territory. They also feared that the company's use of water would have a disastrous effect on the delicate desert aquifers that feed the lake. The people forged coalitions with other Native groups and with environmental organizations, such as the Sierra Club, urging intervention by the federal government. In 2001, the Zunis and their allies formed the Zuni Salt Lake Coalition that organized campaigns against the SRP's plans. They sponsored a relay run from Zuni Pueblo to Phoenix, Arizona, a distance of seven hundred miles round-trip to publicize their cause. Then, in July of 2003, they held a People's Hearing at the Zuni Pueblo to discuss their situation. At the end of the hearing, attended by more than five hundred people, a torrential thunderstorm suddenly appeared, unleashing heavy rains. Since rain has always been understood as an omen from the spirit world, the Zunis interpreted this event as a sign of spiritual support for their cause.

One month later, in August of 2003, SRP management issued a report canceling its plans for the strip mine near Zuni Salt Lake. They stated that they will be obtaining cheaper,

cleaner coal in Wyoming but the pressure and publicity surrounding the Zuni sites must also have had an impact. In the
words of Zuni Pueblo Councilman Carlton Albert: "It has been
a long twenty-year struggle with lots of mental anguish and
frustration for our people, but we have had our voices heard.
There is no word to express our appreciation to those who have
given us help. If there is a lesson to be learned, it is to never give
up and stay focused on what you want to accomplish."
Carmelita Sanchez, the Zuni lieutenant governor, said: "It
seemed like a burden was lifted from my heart and shoulders."
Andy Bessler, an environmental activist working with the Sierra
Club, stressed the ". . . testament to the spirit of the Zuni people, other Native American tribes, and non-Native supporters
who would not relinquish Salt Woman in the name of cheap
coal." Finally, New Mexico Governor Bill Richardson stated: "I
think it's important to protect Native American religious sites."
Zuni Councilman Dan Simplicio concurred: "It's been a
tremendous and costly battle, and I'm glad it's over. The awak-
ening we had for the past two years was really strong. It awak-
ened our powers of spiritual belief."

The Zunis' efforts to protect the Zuni Salt Lake are part of
the efforts of many Native American groups to honor and
maintain lands that they hold sacred. Some of these lands are
believed to be places of origin of the people's ancestors.
Others are thought to be inhabited by spirit beings or contain
shrines where offerings are made to the deities. In a case
related to the issue of sacred sites, the Zuni tribe, along with
the nearby Hopi tribe and the Navajo Nation, won a victory
in the U.S. Court of Appeals for the Ninth Circuit when the
judges issued a ruling that confirmed the actions of Arizona's
Department of Transportation, which had denied permits to a
company seeking to exploit resources on land at Woodruff
Butte, a site held sacred by the Indians. The company, Cholla
Ready Mix, had sought to sell material mined at the butte for
use in building and maintaining roads.

Zuni councilmen Edward Wemytewa and Carlton Albert, along with Zuni Governor Arlen Quetawki, and Ron Solimon, president of the Indian Pueblo Cultural Center, are shown here (left to right) during a press conference in August 2003, after Salt River Project announced that it would not develop a strip mine near Zuni Salt Lake. The Zuni and many other southwestern tribes were determined to stop the construction of the 18,000-acre mine because it would have damaged the lake, disturbed sacred burial sites, and put an end to religious pilgrimages to the sacred site.

The court's decision, rendered in 2004, recognized the "religious, cultural, and historical significance" of the region to the tribes. They based their decision, in part, on the fact that Woodruff Butte is eligible for listing in the National Register of Historic Places. Although the company had argued that by protecting the sites, Arizona was violating the U.S. Constitution's separation of church and state, the judges declared that Arizona was not promoting religion or any particular religion but instead was acting with a "secular purpose" by making sure that state construction projects "do not harm a site of religious, historical, and cultural importance to several Native American groups and the nation as a whole." Furthermore, "Because of the unique status of Native American societies in North American history, protecting Native American shrines and other culturally important sites has historical value for the nation as a whole."

While this ruling applies particularly to Woodruff Butte, it has wider significance because it gives precedence to Native American concerns for their land over those of competing interests when specific cultural meanings can be demonstrated.

Protection of sacred sites is the focus of legislation introduced into Congress in 2003. A proposed law, called the Native American Sacred Lands Act, contains a number of significant features. It protects sacred sites that are located on federally controlled land from development. In order to gain these protections, a Native American tribe would be required to supply evidence that the site in question has been used as part of traditional rituals or cultural practices and that its development would result in significant damage. Of particular importance is the fact that supporting evidence could be in the form of oral history or "Native science," which is defined as

> the oral knowledge of Native Americans gained throughout history by observation and experience; embodies traditional lifestyles and values; is based on the fundamental belief in the sanctity of all life; is guided by principles that include interdependency, reciprocity, and the significance of place; is a living, spiritual knowledge of the relationships between the land, natural resources, and the environment, and is transferred from one generation to the next often through oral tradition and practice.

Recognition of the validity of oral history is an important advance in the protection of Native lands and cultures. It equates Native Americans' knowledge and traditions with scientific or historical documents.

The Native American Sacred Lands Act has been introduced in several sessions of Congress but has yet to be acted upon by the full body. Still, some courts and U.S. government agencies have respected the rights of Native Americans to their sacred sites by banning developments and sporting activities in their vicinity.

In addition to their concerns about protecting sacred sites, the Zunis seek guarantees of respect for cultural resources and cultural knowledge. In testimony before the United States Senate Committee on Indian Affairs in 2002, Zuni Governor Malcolm Bowekaty stressed the People's desire to protect their sacred objects in the places where they are found. Although U.S. government regulations guarantee that objects will not be destroyed when construction or development occurs, the Zunis believe that part of the sacredness of such objects is related to the place in which they are located. That is, since the ancestors and the deities have situated the objects in their specific locations, disturbing them or transporting them elsewhere, violates their sanctity.

The Zunis also want to ensure the privacy of knowledge about ritual and spiritual matters. According to Malcolm Bowekaty's testimony before Congress:

> The Zuni Tribe finds itself in a bind when it comes to the release of esoteric information. While the Federal agencies are very sensitive to our need to protect esoteric information, it is difficult for us to convey the importance of specific cultural resources without giving away information that is esoteric. [For instance] We attempt to explain that a plant is sacred to us without stating why it is sacred to us.

One of the cultural resources recently returned to the Zunis is a collection of pottery taken between 1917 and 1924 by an archaeological expedition investigating the ancient trading center of Hawikkuh. This was a center at an important crossroads to which Native peoples from the Southwest came to

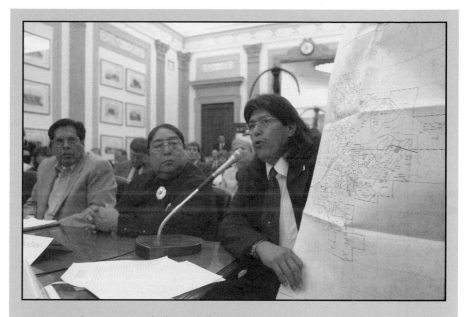

Former Zuni governor Malcolm Bowekaty, who served in that position from 1998 to 2002, helped develop many successful projects during his term, including a major water distribution project. Today, Bowekaty serves as CEO of the Inter-Tribal Economic Alliance (ITEA), which is a nonprofit organization that supports business development in Native American communities. Bowekaty (right) is seen here speaking on behalf of the Zunis during a 2002 Senate Indian Affairs Committee hearing on protecting Native American sacred places.

exchange their goods. Some twenty thousand artifacts were taken out of Hawikuh during the excavation for study and storage at the Smithsonian Institution in Washington D.C. The Zunis have long considered these artifacts to be significant cultural resources documenting their prosperous history and the critical role they played in southwestern trade. In 2002, seventy-five pieces of pottery, representing the stylistic achievements of Zuni artisans, were returned to the Zuni Pueblo and displayed at an exhibition at their A:shiwi A:wan Museum and Heritage Center. Prior to the transfer of pots from the Smithsonian, Eileen Yatsattie, a contemporary Zuni potter, traveled to Washington, D.C., to advise the museum's staff concerning the cleaning and care of the pots.

In consultation about another critical issue, the Zunis signed an agreement in 2004 with Gale Norton, the secretary of the Department of Interior, that settled a controversy about water rights. The agreement concerns water levels in "Zuni Heaven," a sacred land believed by the Zunis to be the place of connection between the everyday world of the living and the spirit world of the dead and of the deities. The area, once filled with "waist deep, swift moving streams" according to Zuni elders, is now virtually dry due primarily to the construction of dams upstream that have diverted water. According to the terms of the agreement, the Zunis can have access to up to 3,600 acre-feet of water and up to 1,500 acre-feet from wells. This will help the Zunis in their attempts to return the area to its former wetlands condition. According to Wilford Eriacho, chairman of the Zuni water rights negotiating team, "They are the most important lands from time immemorial. The water rights settlement will start to ease the hearts and minds of the Zuni people." Secretary of Interior Gale Norton said: "It's important to protect and restore a sacred area. We need to have traditions that are long-standing and for our cultures to remain vibrant. Today's event has great significance for the cultural and natural future of the Southwest."

This settlement comes with a price tag of $19.2 million to be paid by the federal government, while the State of Arizona will contribute $1.6 million. With the money, the Zunis will establish a Zuni Indian Tribe Water Rights Development Fund with which to restore the land and purchase additional water rights.

In addition to securing water rights for sacred lands, the Zunis are moving forward with programs aimed at developing sustainable agriculture projects on their reservation. For example, they are utilizing traditional techniques such as "brush and rock structures" that keep back the rushing waters that occur when torrential summer rains hit the dry land. Although Zuni farming is dependent on rainfall, too much sudden water can destroy their crops. The structures, made by piling flat heavy rocks on top of juniper and sagebrush placed at the bottom of a gully, also retard soil erosion and retain water needed to irrigate the fields. These traditional methods of conserving water and protecting fields work as well, and sometimes better, than modern structures. Of course, they cost less.

Although the Zunis are proud of their age-old knowledge, they also adapt new technologies, using computers and sophisticated mapping techniques to record soil and weather conditions and monitor crop production. Among the main goals are protection of the Zuni watershed, rehabilitating traditional peach orchards, and developing wetlands as habitats for fish and wildlife. Monitoring and conserving rangeland and grazing territories for sheep, goats, and cattle are additional important tasks. Finally, protecting forest resources will help ensure their continuation for future generations.

Many of the economic plans of the Zuni tribe are dedicated to the interests of local farmers and herders in part because of their important contribution to the Zuni economy and in part because they are continuing an ancient tradition of land use. But the Zunis are also protecting their economic interest in making jewelry and other crafts for sale. They were in the forefront of calling for federal legislation to protect authentic Native American craftspeople. The Zunis, along with their Hopi and Navajo neighbors, formed the Council for Indigenous Arts and Culture, based at the Zuni Reservation, to protect their cultural, artistic, and commercial interests. As a result of pressure from Native groups, in 1990 the U.S. Congress passed the Indian Arts and Crafts Act, making it illegal to sell any art or craft product "in a manner that falsely suggests it is Indian produced, an Indian product, or the product of a particular Indian or Indian tribe or Indian arts and crafts organization." The Act is aimed at protecting Native American artisans and the authenticity of their work. The legislation is a response to the proliferation of the illegal sale of jewelry falsely

labeled as authentic Indian. Much of the fake jewelry is produced abroad, made by workers receiving low wages and using
inferior materials. When these items are sold in the United
States at low prices, they undercut the value of authentic works,
which, because of the skill of Native artisans and the high quality of their materials, naturally cost more.

Although some Zunis pursue traditional roles as farmers
and herders and others are involved in the arts, most people
earn their income from wages in a wide variety of occupations.
According to statistics collected in 2000 by the U.S. Census
Bureau, 50.8 percent of the reservation population aged 16
years or older were in the labor force. Of those, 41.1 percent
were employed while 9.8 percent were unemployed. Statistics
also illustrated that 49.2 percent were officially classified as
"not in the labor force," meaning that they were no longer
actively seeking work, possibly because they did not intend to
work or because they were discouraged due to a lack of available jobs. The statistics on employment were roughly the same
for men and women. These figures indicate a relative disad-
vantage for Zunis when compared with other residents of the
State of New Mexico or the nation as a whole as the following
table shows:

	Percent Employed	Percent Unemployed	Percent Not in Labor Force
Zunis	50.8%	9.8%	49.2%
New Mexico	60.0%	4.8%	35.2%
United States	67.1%	4.2%	32.9%

Analyzed by "class of work," the largest category is that of
government employment. That is, 43.8 percent of Zunis who
are employed are working for some government agency, either

federal or local. In addition, 35.8 percent are privately employed while 20.2 percent are self-employed in their own businesses.

Within types of occupations, the largest percentage of Zuni workers (32.4 percent) are listed as working in "educational, health and social services." Other statistically significant occupations include manufacturing, public administration, retail trade, and construction. Only 1.7 percent of the Zunis are engaged in agriculture, forestry, mining, and fishing and hunting.

Consistent with the difficulty of finding jobs on or near their reservation, household and family incomes for the Zunis tend to be lower than for other residents of New Mexico or the nation, as indicated in the following table:

	Median Family Income	Per-Capita Income
Zunis	$22,067	$6,908
New Mexico	$30,836	$21,164
United States	$46,737	$27,203

These data show that the Zuni family income is less than half that of other United States residents, while the Zuni per-capita income is about one quarter that of other Americans. The fact the Zunis' per-capita income is much lower relative to the United States in general than their family income (one quarter rather than one half) reflects the larger size of Zuni families than is the general American norm. Indeed, the median family size for the United States is 2.59 persons, but the Zunis have an average family size of 4.54 persons, nearly double the American norm. The Zuni pattern is consistent with that of Native Americans living on reservations.

Income is obviously related to statistics on poverty. As a

consequence of their low incomes, Zunis experience relatively greater levels of poverty than do other Americans:

	Percentage of Individuals in Poverty
Zunis	43.0%
New Mexico	19.3%
United States	23.7%

The Zunis therefore are more than three times as likely to live in poverty as are other Americans and more than twice as likely to live in poverty as are other residents of New Mexico.

Statistical information concerning educational attainment for Zunis indicates a somewhat lower percentage of high school graduates than the national norm but a much lower percentage of college or university graduates. The following table displays the relevant data:

	Percentage High School Graduate	Percentage College Graduate
Zunis	63.7%	5.7%
New Mexico	75.1%	20.4%
United States	75.2%	20.3%

Another 22.1 percent of Zunis have attended some college classes but have not received degrees, while 4.7 percent have their associate's degree. Still, with lower rates of educational attainment, Zunis may lack some of the literacy and mathematical skills necessary for certain kinds of occupations,

In 2003, Governor Bill Richardson appointed Carlotta Penny Bird (shown here) as New Mexico's assistant secretary for Indian education. Penny Bird is actively working to improve the percentage of Zuni high school graduates, which stood at 63.7 percent in 2000, more than 11 percent below the state average of 75.1 percent.

particularly those jobs paying higher wages. These data partially explain, or are at least consistent with, the data on employment and income.

Despite the lack of well-paying jobs in their own community, the population of the Zuni Reservation has continued to increase, a steady growth throughout the twentieth century. According to official U.S. Census Bureau figures for the year 2000, the number of people enrolled as members of the Zuni tribe stood at 10,122. Of these, 9,094 identified themselves as members of one tribe, while the remainder reported belonging to more than one Native group. However, the population of the Zuni Reservation was 6,367. Nearly all residents of the reservation are Zunis (97.4 percent). Most of the other residents are either white or Hispanic. These data together indicate that about two thirds of the registered Zunis live on their reservation while about one third live away. Rates of outmigration from reservations throughout the United States vary considerably. The patterns for the Zunis are certainly within the norm and perhaps reflect a somewhat greater than average tendency to live on the reservation.

The Zuni population is fairly representative of the gender percentages in the country as a whole, having 3,304 females and 3,063 males (51.9 percent to 48.1 percent). The Zunis differ from general U.S. communities, however, in being a relatively young population. Their median age is 28.6 years, while the median age in the United States is 35. The youthful age structure of the Zuni Reservation is a consequence of having relatively large families, at least as compared to other Americans.

The vast majority of Zunis live in households with family members (89.7 percent). Only 9.0 percent of Zuni households consist of one person living alone, while another 1.3 percent of households consist of people living together who are not members of the same family.

An interesting insight into Zuni family organization is the fact that in 48.9 percent of extended family households where grandparents are present and where there are children under the age of 18, the grandparents are responsible as caregivers for their grandchildren. That is, grandparents are not merely additional residents of the households but are significant caretakers and as such are integral to the activities and functioning of the family.

Taken together, data on population trends and household composition indicate a strong sense of community and belonging. While there are economic difficulties due to the lack of jobs, people choose to remain on the reservation because of the sense of security and comfort afforded by living amongst a group with whom one develops a positive and nurturing identity.

This identity is reflected, in part, in a vibrant tradition of maintaining the native Zuni language. According to U.S. Census Bureau data, an impressive 85.7 percent of Zunis speak their indigenous language at home, while 14.3 percent speak English only. Most of the Zuni speakers are bilinguals, able to converse in both Zuni and English, but 29.2 percent report that they speak English "less than very well." Additional data on language indicate that the Zuni language is spoken by people in every age category, including a large number of young children. The census reports that 1,818 children between the ages of 5 and 17 are fluent speakers of Zuni, thus ensuring continuation of the language into future generations, because it is the number of children speaking a language that reflects its vitality. These data contrast with trends for other Native American languages still spoken in the United States, indicating that only a small number of languages have a significant group of young speakers and therefore most Native languages will probably not be maintained much into the future.

In addition to their concerns about their land, economic development, and cultural rights, the Zunis are concerned about the health problems of their community. Doctors and researchers have focused on the very high levels of kidney disease and renal failure among Zunis. In particular, a study conducted in 1985 revealed that 1.6 percent of Zunis had renal disease, a figure that was 14 times the rate for U.S. whites and three times the rates for other Native Americans. Zunis of all ages, from young children to the elderly, are affected. About one third of the cases of kidney disease were connected to diabetes but the remainder, a majority, were of unknown cause. A number of theories have been proposed, but none is certain. One theory suggests a genetic component, because there are strong family clusters of the disease and the Zuni community tends to be ethnically homogeneous. Another theory suggests some environmental causes or contributing factors, such as exposure to possibly toxic materials associated with making jewelry or pottery, or to some toxins in the water or salt consumed by the people.

Because of the seriousness of these ailments, the Zuni Pueblo Council has agreed to cooperate with the Genetics Institute to study the prevalence of the disease among their people. By 2004, interviewers had spoken with nearly every member of the Zuni community. Researchers are collecting samples of DNA from many members in order to uncover any genetic factors that may predispose a person to develop kidney disease. They have also agreed to return all DNA samples to the Zuni community to establish a repository that will form the basis of future medical research on this and other ailments affecting the people.

As in all societies, there are differences of opinion among Zunis about how best to strengthen their community, which paths to take for economic development, and how to merge tradition and change. These issues are discussed and debated at public meetings, as well as through conversations in a local paper formed in 1998, called the *Shiwi Messenger*, which prints news stories and opinion pieces for the interchange of ideas.

The Zunis have demonstrated a remarkable ability to withstand centuries of intense pressure, first from Spanish invaders and even more from agents of U.S. control. Government officials, military, missionaries, and teachers attempted to alter indigenous ways of life and systems of ethics. Of course, much of Zuni activities have changed, as they have for all peoples. But a solid core of Zuni values and attitudes has remained strong, transmitted within families and in the community as a whole from generation to generation. In the words of James Enote, Project Leader of the Zuni Conservation Project and head of the Department of Natural Resources:

> For thousands of years we Zunis have lived in a complex and delicate environment which has sustained our ancestors and which continues to bring great benefits to our people today. But with the continuing growth of our population and the increasing demand for limited not sure resources, the time has come to decide what means we will use to ensure that the resources and benefits available to our ancestors will be available for future generations.

Thinking about these issues is of paramount importance to Zunis as they look to the new century. As Enote concludes, summing up the needs to both conserve their land and resources and develop their economy:

> Today Zuni could be described as both a developing nation and a prosperous community. Our contemporary habits are approaching the patterns of the United States in general, but our culture and ways of life remain consistently and uniquely Zuni. We are faced with the enormous challenge of moving into the next century maintaining our traditions and values, yet needing the modern technical capability to deal with the conservation and development issues that confront us.

The Zunis at a Glance

Tribe Zuni

Culture Area Southwest

Geography New Mexico

Linguistic Family Possibly Penutian

Current Population (2000) More than 10,000

First European Contact Estevanico, Spanish, 1539

Federal Status Tribal reservation in New Mexico

A.D. **700/800** Zunis' ancestors settle in their present-day territory, establishing several towns, most inhabited by about one hundred people.

1300s Six Zuni villages, including Hawikuh, a major center for intertribal trade in the Southwest, are established.

1539 Franciscan priest Marcos de Niza sent by the viceroy of the Spanish colony in Mexico to explore the American Southwest. Although he never met the Zunis, he claimed to have found wealthy cities, part of an empire he called the Seven Cities of Cibola; the expedition led by Francisco Vasquez de Coronado arrives in Zuni territory.

1540 The first battle between the Spanish invaders and the Zunis defending their villages; Coronado leaves Zuni territory and sets up headquarters of the new Spanish colony in the Pueblo village of Tiguex on the Rio Grande in New Mexico.

1632 Permanent Catholic missions in two Zuni villages established, but Zunis continue to resist Spanish colonial control.

1680 Zunis join other Puebloan peoples in the Pueblo Revolt, killing their resident priests, burning church buildings, and expelling Spanish settlers who had intruded on their land. As a defensive measure, the Zunis abandone their villages and move to a settlement on top of a mesa called Dowa Yallane, where they remain for fifteen years.

1692 The Spanish reenter the Southwest from Mexico and regain control of most of the Puebloan towns along the Rio Grande. However, the Zunis continue to successfully resist complete Spanish control.

Late **1600s** Zunis begin to adopt some elements of Spanish economy, particularly sheep and horses.

1705 The Zunis sign an agreement of friendship with the Spanish; the Zunis agreed to allow some Spanish presence in their territory in exchange for promises of protection from Apache and Navajo raiders.

1821 Mexican independence results in a shift in formal governance of Zuni territory from Spain to Mexico.

1848 Treaty of Guadalupe Hidalgo signed, ending war between the United States and Mexico and transferring southwestern territory (the present-day states of New Mexico and Arizona) to the United States.

1863 President Abraham Lincoln presents a ceremonial cane to the Zuni governor, Mariano, as a sign of friendship.

1877 Zuni Reservation created by an Executive Order of President Rutherford B. Hayes; the reservation is only about one tenth the size of Zuni territory before the European invasions.

1883 A second Executive Order is signed, adding some outlying areas to the reservation.

1897 The first government-run day school opens on the Zuni Reservation.

1917 An Executive Order by President Woodrow Wilson adds approximately 80,000 acres to the Zuni Reservation. Additional parcels of land are added in 1935 and 1940, bringing the total to approximately 400,000 acres.

1934 The Stock Reduction Program, instituted by the Bureau of Indian Affairs, divides the Zuni Reservation into eighteen grazing units, each given a quota of livestock, and forces Zuni herders to reduce their stock of sheep.

1970 Zunis adopt a formal constitution with a Zuni Tribal Council as their official legislative and executive body.

1976 The Zuni Range Code, regulating livestock holdings is created.

1977 The Zuni radio station KSHI-FM is founded.

1978 Zunis obtain a lease to land surrounding their Zuni Salt Lake, located fifty miles southeast of their reservation.

1984 The Zunis win the return of Koluwala-wa, a sacred land that was the site of pilgrimages for rain and good crops.

1987   The U.S. Court of Indian Claims grants the Zunis title to a large portion of present-day Arizona and New Mexico, stating that the tribe had been wrongfully deprived of nearly 15 million acres of land, and awards them $25 million as compensation.

1990   The federal Native American Graves Protection and Repatriation Act passed after years of work by the Zunis to secure the return of some of their sacred objects; passage of the Zuni Land Conservation Act, which establishes a permanent Zuni Indian Resource Development Trust Fund of $17 million to implement the Zuni Sustainable Resource Development Plan, is overseen by the Zuni Conservation Project; passage of the Indian Arts and Crafts Act intends to protect the authenticity of Native American jewelry and other craft products; formation of the Council for Indigenous Arts and Culture, based at the Zuni Reservation.

1992   Zunis successfully repatriate sixty-three sacred objects previously held by museums in Washington D.C., New York, and Albuquerque, New Mexico.

1998   The first Zuni newspaper, the *Shiwi Messenger*, established.

2002   Zuni Governor Malcolm Bowekaty testifies at the U.S. Senate Committee on Indian Affairs about the Zunis' desire to protect sacred objects and cultural resources; Zunis receive seventy-five pieces of pottery taken in the early twentieth century from the Zuni village of Hawikuh, a major intertribal trading center from the thirteenth into the sixteenth century.

2003   In response to Zuni protests, the Salt River Project, a private utility company, abandons its plan to develop mining on land surrounding the sacred Zuni Salt Lake.

2004   The U.S. Court of Appeals for the Ninth Circuit issues a ruling protecting sacred land at Woodruff Butte from mining and economic development proposed by the Cholla Ready Mix company; Zunis sign an agreement with the Department of Interior granting the Zunis 3,600 acre-feet of water to help restore water levels in "Zuni Heaven."

agent—A person appointed by the Bureau of Indian Affairs to supervise U.S. government programs on a reservation and/or in a specific region.

Awonawilona—The deity, who is both male and female, responsible for creating the universe.

Bow Priesthood—A prestigious group whose members were responsible for carrying out warfare and keeping order in the villages.

Bureau of Indian Affairs (BIA)—A federal government agency, now within the Department of the Interior, founded to manage relations with Native American tribes.

clan—A multigenerational group having a shared identity, organization, and property based on belief in their descent from a common ancestor. Because clan members consider themselves closely related, marriage within a clan is strictly prohibited.

culture—The learned behavior of humans; nonbiological, socially taught activities; the way of life of a group of people.

ethnologist—An anthropologist who specializes in comparing and analyzing different cultures.

fetish—A representative image of a deity made of wood and decorated with paint and feathers. Besides being a work of art, a fetish has great religious significance.

Indian Reorganization Act (IRA)—The 1934 federal law that ended the policy of allotting plots of land to individuals and encouraged the development of reservation communities. The act also provided for the creation of autonomous tribal governments.

itiwana—The middle place of the world, where the Zunis were told to settle after emerging from the inside of the earth in their creation legend.

kachinas—Souls of the dead who are impersonated by Zunis wearing special costumes and performing elaborate public dances. All Zuni men were members of one of the six kachina societies.

kiva—A special square-shaped room, entered by a ladder through the ceiling, where religious ceremonies are held.

Koyemshi—An ancient group of Raw People who are impersonated throughout the year. Also called the Mudheads, each Koyemshi acts like a clown but is considered to have great power to bring good fortune and rain.

lhamana—A Zuni man who wore the clothing and performed the work traditionally associated with women. Lhamana (also known as berdaches) were considered by tribal members to be of a third gender, distinct from both males and females.

matrilineal—A kinship system based on descent from the woman's lineage.

Meriam Report—A U.S. government study in 1928 that found appalling conditions of poverty on many reservations and suggested increased federal funding to Native American tribes.

metate—A specialized grinding stone for making meal out of seeds, nuts, and corn.

Native American Graves Protection and Repatriation Act of 1990—A Congressional resolution that allows Native American tribes to repossess the artifacts and grave remains that were taken from them by museums and individual collectors.

Neweekwe—Members of a Zuni medicine society who specialize in curing stomach ailments; the Neweekwes engage in sophisticated forms of clowning.

pekwin—The head of Zuni village government who was appointed by the council of priests and worked with them to manage collective work, community affairs, and religious ceremonies. The pekwin was required to be a member of the Dogwood clan, as well as a kind and respected individual.

Rain Priesthood—The most powerful priesthood, whose members derived their knowledge and powers from the Rain-Bringing Spirits and who performed rituals that would bring rain to the Zunis.

Raw People—The many powerful deities and spirits in the Zuni religion, named for the raw food given to them as offerings from humans. The Zunis also say prayers and perform rituals in the Raw People's honor, and in exchange the Raw People provide protection and good fortune.

reservation—A tract of land retained by Indians for their own occupation and use.

Shalakos—Six powerful, birdlike beings who are impersonated by select Zuni men every fall and bring abundant crops and many children.

tribe—A society consisting of several separate communities united by kinship, culture, language, and other social institutions, including clans, religious organizations, and warrior societies.

Treaty of Guadalupe Hidalgo—The treaty that ended the Mexican War in 1848 and granted the United States ownership of present-day Arizona and New Mexico. In the treaty, the U.S. government promised to respect the land and rights of the native peoples in the region.

Zuni Land Conservation Act of 1990—As settlement of a Zuni lawsuit against the federal government, Congress established the permanent Zuni Indian Resource Development Trust Fund of $17 million. Interest from the fund supports the Zuni Sustainable Resource Development Plan.

Zuni Tribal Council—Recognized by the U.S. government in the early 1970s, the Zunis' official legislative and executive body has the right to control the local government and organize elections.

Books

Crampton, C. Gregory. *The Zunis of Cibola*. Salt Lake City, Utah: University of Utah Press, 1977.

Cushing, Frank Hamilton. *Cushing at Zuni: The Correspondence and Journals of Frank Hamilton Cushing 1879–1884*, edited by Jesse Green. Albuquerque, N.M.: University of New Mexico Press, 1990.

———. *Zuni Folk Tales*. 1901. Reprint. Tucson, Ariz.: University of Arizona Press, 1986.

———. *Zuni: Selected Writings of Frank Hamilton Cushing*, edited by Jesse Green. Lincoln, Nebr.: University of Nebraska Press, 1979.

Dozier, Edward. *The Pueblo Indians of North America*. New York: Holt, Rinehart & Winston, 1970.

Ferguson, T.J., and E.R. Hart. *A Zuni Atlas*. Norman, Okla.: University of Oklahoma Press, 1985.

Hart, E. Richard, ed. *Zuni and the Courts: A Struggle for Sovereign Land Rights*. Lawrence, Kans.: University Press of Kansas, 1995.

Morris, John Miller. *From Coronado to Escalante: The Explorers of the Spanish Southwest*. New York: Chelsea House, 1992.

Ortiz, Alfonso, ed. *Handbook of North American Indians. Southwest*. Vol. 9. Washington, D.C.: Smithsonian Institution, 1979.

———. *The Pueblo*. New York: Chelsea House, 1994.

Ostler, James. *Zuni: A Village of Silversmiths*. Zuni, N.M.: A:Shiwi Publishers, 1996.

Pollock, Penny. *The Turkey Girl: A Zuni Cinderella Story*. Boston, Mass.: Little, Brown, 1996.

Tedlock, Barbara. *The Beautiful and the Dangerous: Encounters with the Zuni Indians*. New York: Viking, 1992.

Wilson, Edmund. *Red, Black, Blond and Olive: Studies in Four Civilizations: Zuni, Haiti, Soviet Russia, Israel*. New York: Oxford University Press, 1956.

Wright, Barton. *Kachinas of the Zuni*. Flagstaff, Ariz.: Northland Press, 1985.

Wyaco, Virgil. *A Zuni Life: A Pueblo Indian in Two Worlds*. Albuquerque, N.M.: Side Canyon Press, 2004.

The Zuni People. *Zunis: Self-Portrayals*. Translated by Alvian Quam. Albuquerque, N.M.: University of New Mexico Press, 1972.

Websites

Pueblo of Zuni
http://www.ashiwi.net/

Information on the Zunis
http://www.crystalinks.com/zuni.html

Zuni Origin Story
http://www.sacred-texts.com/nam/zuni/ bunzel/zom.htm

A:shiwi A:wan Museum and Heritage Center
http://www.wnmu.org/mcf/museums/ ashiwi.html

page:

6: © CORBIS

11: Courtesy Museum of New Mexico, Neg. No. 144511

18: Keystone View Co., Courtesy Museum of New Mexico, Neg. No. 89328

24: Ben Wittick, Courtesy Museum of New Mexico, Neg. No. 16068

30: Courtesy Museum of New Mexico, Neg. No. 2565

34: © CORBIS

40: Edward S. Curtis, Courtesy Museum of New Mexico, Neg. No. 144509

45: Courtesy Museum of New Mexico, Neg. No. 47996

52: Smithsonian Institution, Neg. No. 2267.E

61: Keystone View Co., Courtesy Museum of New Mexico, Neg. No 89327

65: John. K. Hillers, Courtesty Museum of New Mexico, Neg. No. 73898

69: © Christie's Images/CORBIS

78: Jesse L. Nusbaum, Courtesy Museum of New Mexico, Neg. No. 61740

84: © Peter Lamb

88: Frasher, Courtesy Museum of New Mexico, Neg. No. 9189

95: © Titus Paulsel/PhotoCorral.com

98: Associated Press, AP

101: Associated Press, AP

107: Associated Press, AP

A: Department of Material Culture, Colorado Historical Society, CHS-X3071

B: Department of Material Culture, Colorado Historical Society, CHS-X2925

C: Department of Material Culture, Colorado Historical Society, CHS-X3290

D: Department of Material Culture, Colorado Historical Society, CHS-X3073

E: Department of Material Culture, Colorado Historical Society, CHS-X32421

F: Western History/Genealogy Department, Denver Public Library

G: © Bildarchiv Preussischer Kulturbesitz/Art Resource, NY

H: © Time Life Pictures/Getty Images

Cover: Department of Material Culture, Colorado Historical Society, CHS-X2817

Nancy Bonvillain, Ph.D., is currently a visiting faculty member in the summer session at Columbia University and teaches anthropology and linguistics at Simon's Rock College of Bard in Great Barrington, Massachusetts. She has written more than a dozen books including volumes in Chelsea House's INDIANS OF NORTH AMERICA series (*The Huron, Mohawk, Hopi, Teton Sioux, Haida, Sac* and *Fox, Inuit, Santee Sioux, Native American Religion* and *Native American Medicine*). She has also written two volumes of Native American biographies, *Hiawatha* and *Black Hawk*, in the NORTH AMERICAN INDIANS OF ACHIEVEMENT series.

Dr. Bonvillain's concentrations within the field have been in Native American studies and in linguistics. She has carried out fieldwork in the Navajo Nation in Arizona and the Akwesasne Mohawk Reserve in Ontario/Quebec and New York. Her dissertation was a study of the Mohawk language as spoken at the Akwesasne Reserve. She has also prepared a Mohawk/English dictionary and book of conversations for use at the schools on the reserve.

Ada E. Deer is the director of the American Indian Studies program at the University of Wisconsin–Madison. She was the first woman to serve as chair of her tribe, the Menominee Nation, the first woman to head the Bureau of Indian Affairs in the U.S. Department of the Interior, and the first American Indian woman to run for Congress and secretary of state of Wisconsin. Deer has also chaired the Native American Rights Fund, coordinated workshops to train American Indian women as leaders, and championed Indian participation in the Peace Corps. She holds degrees in social work from Wisconsin and Columbia.